THE BATH
SHORT STORY
AWARD
ANTHOLOGY
2014

THE BATH SHORT STORY AWARD ANTHOLOGY 2014

Compiled by
Jude Higgins, Jane Riekemann
and Anna Schlesinger

BROWN
DOG
BOOKS

Published under licence by Brown Dog Books and The Self Publishing Partnership
7 Green Park Station, Bath BA1 1JB

www.selfpublishingpartnership.co.uk

ISBN printed book: 978-1-903056-84-4
ISBN e-book: 978-1-903056-85-1

Cover design by Elinor Nash

Printed and bound by CPI Group (UK) Ltd, Croydon CR0 4YY

CONTENTS

Introduction
Jude Higgins, Jane Riekemann & Anna Schlesinger VII

Additional acknowledgements IX

2014 Judge Lucy Luck X

The Ghost Boy Elinor Nash **1**

The Beautiful Thing Kit de Waal **10**

No Man's Land Alex Hammond **18**

The Language of Birds Anne Corlett **24**

It's a Girl Lisa Harding **34**

Under the Jasmine Tree Roisín O'Donnell **42**

The Crust Mona Porte **51**

Zoom Emily Bullock **60**

Pretending to Know the Words Helen Cooper **67**

Greta Garbo and the Chrysanthemum Man K M Elkes **75**

The Radiant Girl Barbara Featherstone **80**

Nothing Stays the Same Alison Fisher **88**

Eighty-Six Teaspoons Eamonn Griffin **96**

Guy Ropes Ledlowe Guthrie **104**

Ghost Bike Sophie Hampton **113**

In Her Hair Claire Hynes **121**

Clairol Perfect 10, 9a K Lockwood Jefford **130**

Teodor's Boots Karen Jones **138**

Gon-Do-La Annemarie Neary **146**

Charade Samuel Wright **154**

INTRODUCTION

The Bath Short Story Award is only in its second year but, once again, attracted entries from all over the world – this time 1000. Whittling them down to a longlist of 40 proved a real challenge to us and to our team of readers, most of whom are also writers. We all had our favourites but the ones that made it to the longlist were endorsed by at least three of the team while the shortlist was selected by us. And, of course, Lucy Luck had the challenging task of picking the outright winners. We thank her for her shrewd judgements, insightful comments and tremendous enthusiasm and support.

The stories we chose for the anthology come from both the short and longlist. They reflect a range of historical and contemporary themes such as the effects of war, coping with loss and struggles in relationships. They combine marvellous storytelling with inventive language and style, as well as offering unusual angles on enduring themes. There is a variety of genres: this year magical realism features along with drama, comedy and fable. The stories indicate, in often poignant and ironic ways, the frailty and absurdity of human experience and writers demonstrate great skill to show these elements in up to 2200 words. We feel the stories here will continue to resonate long after the first reading.

We're excited to be producing our second anthology. Many of last year's winning stories were featured in Good Reads published by Hearst Magazines and are still available on Amazon for Kindle or ebook downloads. This year we opted to go for print and digital versions and hope you find reading the words of so many talented writers a rich and rewarding experience. We're thrilled by the cover of the anthology, designed and produced by Elinor Nash, our first prize winner, who is an extremely talented artist as well as a writer.

Thanks also to Mr B's Emporium of Books, one of Bath's exciting independent book stores, who sponsored our local prize. We greatly appreciate Alex Wilson, co-founder of Writing Events Bath, for suggesting a prize for an unpublished writer, and Writing Events Bath for sponsoring the Acorn Award. We love having the Acorn finials on the Circus building in Bath as part of our logo, and Elinor's version, in paint and collage, makes this symbol of creative growth even more special.

The 2015 Bath Short Story Award opens on November 1st. One of our aims in founding the competition was to help short story writers flourish and receive recognition so we were delighted to receive a ringing endorsement at this year's London Short Story Festival in June. At one event, 'The Short Story Gatekeepers' chaired by Vanessa Gebbie, the entire panel, consisting of a literary agent, several editors, a representative from Booktrust and a BBC Radio 4 producer, was unanimous in stressing the importance of writing awards such as ours for discovering writers. The shortlists of regional, national and international competitions are examined to find the powerful, resonant voices of tomorrow. It is wonderful to be part of this process.

Jude Higgins, Jane Riekemann and Anna Schlesinger

www.bathshortstoryaward.co.uk
Twitter: @BathStoryAward

ADDITIONAL ACKNOWLEDGEMENTS

Our great team of readers for the 2014 award were:

Mina Bancheva
Daisy Behagg
Nina MacPherson
Katharina Riekemann
Hannah Riekemann
Natasha Underwood
William Wright

We thank them for their dedication and enthusiasm.

2014 JUDGE
LUCY LUCK

We were thrilled that Lucy Luck of Lucy Luck Associates Literary Agency agreed to act as our shortlist judge. Lucy is a great supporter of the short story genre and represents several significant short story writers including Kevin Barry (winner of the 2012 Sunday Times EFG Private Bank Short Story Award, as well as other major awards for his novels) and Colin Barrett who recently won the Frank O'Connor Short Story Prize and the Rooney Prize for his debut collection.

Her career in publishing began in 1997 and she worked for over 8 years at Rogers, Coleridge and White Ltd. In 2006, she set up Lucy Luck Associates, an agency focusing on writers of quality fiction and non-fiction, and in 2008 she joined with Aitken Alexander Associates as an associate agency. Other authors she represents include Catherine O' Flynn (winner of the Costa First Novel Award 2007 and Galaxy Newcomer of the Year), Adam Thorpe, Amanda Smyth, Jess Richards, Richard Beard, Owen Martell, Ray Robinson, Greg Baxter, Jon Hotten and John Hooper. She works in association with Aitken Alexander Associates for Foreign, Film & TV rights.

Lucy's comments on the shortlisted and winning entries can be seen at the end of the authors' biographies but overall she said, *'Some very good stories here, all high quality and the judging has been very difficult.'*

FIRST PRIZE
ELINOR NASH

The Ghost Boy

The irregular drumbeat delighted Jake Bennett with its marshmallow sound. From his special blue chair in the overfull living room, each bam-bam-te-bam brought the pinky white balls flashing into view then out again, into view then out.

'Ugh, my head.'

Jake smiled at his mother and began to rock his own head side-bam to side-bam, trying to catch in his open mouth the here then gone again marshmallows.

He knew they weren't real marshmallows. Jake wasn't a fool, despite what some people thought – strangers mostly, with veiled eyes and overloud voices. These marshmallow beats were a gift given to him on the day he turned from a Hardy Teenager racing his bike to school to an upside-down Ghost Boy.

Marshmallow beats weren't the only gifts. There was the

custard swirl of the fan, looping from left to right, the grass green zigzags of rain against the window, the scurrying crimson dashes of his dad turning the pages of the newspaper. Jake sometimes yelled for the place to be quiet just so he could see his smoky grey breathing.

After several more minutes of marshmallow beats, Jake's vision filled with the horror of the vacuum cleaner. Jake hated the vacuum's orange squash sound. The colour leeched into those delicious marshmallow beats and made them sticky.

Jake tried to not let it upset him. When Jake got upset his otherwise weak legs got upset which made his feet kick out which ultimately upset whoever happened to be near them. As the whirr of vacuum continued, Jake felt the upset travel from his crying eyes down to the elasticated waistband of his dark blue jeans. Jake tried to stop the upset trickling down his legs but his mother yanked the vacuum cleaner next to him and – flick – he kicked the upset right into her shin.

Jake often thought his mother was made of glass – the thin frail glass that had shattered around Jake when his world had spun upside-down. She was jagged like glass: sharp elbows and knees and hips and cheekbones. She was transparent like glass. Jake could peer inside and see her slow-beating heart, her broccoli lungs, her china bones. She could break like glass – crash – with one kick of his upset foot.

His dad wasn't glass. His dad was wood, solid and knotted and unmoving. Jake's foot didn't kick his dad so often. It hurt Jake's foot to do it and the upset would bounce back along Jake's legs and up his tummy and it would taste sour in his mouth and then Jake's upset would send him spinning upside-down, over and over like a recurring nightmare and he'd cry out in a pool of sweat.

The marshmallow beat continued and Jake, who'd stopped crying (having kicked the upset to his mother, whose lavender sniffs seemed to Jake to alternate with the drumbeat) listened and watched, no longer trying to catch the marshmallows in his open mouth. He listened and watched until the lavender sniffs went away and his mother helped him to his wheelie-walker which he pushed along to the newly fitted bathroom.

The bathroom used to be upstairs which had given his mother Terrible Backache. After long discussions about money and builders and other things that Jake couldn't help overhearing, a man called Gary came for several weeks and made lots of blood-red star bangs and strange lemon yellow whooshes and (Jake's favourite sound) the indigo velvet spiral of the drill. Gary came into the living room especially to show Jake the drill and the hammer and the screwdriver. Gary told Jake about the new pipes he had to fit and where the stopcock was and the amazing toilet which washed the sitter afterwards. Jake listened and gave Gary his best smile because he liked Gary and the interesting noises Gary made and he especially liked the idea of the toilet which would wash him every time he used it.

His mother readied her hands as Jake manoeuvred himself onto the new shower seat but he could manage well enough. The shower, like the rain, fell in grass green zigzags and washed the stickiness from Jake. It felt so much better than the old bath which had given his mother the Terrible Backache as Jake was a big boy and very heavy and his mother was fragile glass.

Jake's mother wrapped him up in a fluffy towel and he noticed the marshmallow beats had stopped which meant his sister, Ava, had stopped drumming. He had a vague notion of what the drums looked like, metallic blue and silver, but as they were upstairs in what was Jake's old bedroom, he now only ever heard them. He'd like to watch Ava play and have the drumbeat so loud the marshmallows would be twice as big.

Ava was younger than Jake by something less than two years but more than one and she had the same mousy-coloured hair as Jake and the same mousy-coloured eyes as their mother. She was, every day and by little but significant increments, growing more and more like their mother. Jake kept the observation to himself, aware that telling Ava about this growing resemblance would make her screw up her face and send her skin a ghostlier pale, the way it did when she had to help Jake with his breakfast in the morning.

Jake had flashes of memory, like the here-then-gone-again marshmallow beats. In those flashes he saw a small Ava cuddled up on the sofa with their mother. He saw Ava's feet, and his own, sinking in the sand as a wave drew back. He could stand once, unaided, he knew because of the wave memory and because of the dance memory, where he had moved his feet side to side opposite a pretty girl who made his tummy flutter. But that was when he was a Hardy Teenager who could race his bike to school.

In pyjamas now, and back in his special blue chair, Jake saw the light outside fading. His neck wasn't very strong so he rested his head on the high-backed chair and looked ceiling-ward. This meant he only really saw the ever-changing sky out of the sitting room window. The fading light told Jake his dad would be home soon.

'Hey Jakey,' Ava sing-sang and swooped her face into view. Jake said hey Ava and gave her his best smile because she'd brought him his ball which was squashy in his hand and if he squeezed it hard enough – which Jake could sometimes do and sometimes couldn't – the ball vibrated and played a little tune. The tune was the colour of baked beans and he liked the tickly vibration on his palm.

When Jake's hand was too weak to squeeze the ball, Ava squeezed it for him even though she didn't like the tune the colour of baked beans and called it 'annoying.' Sometimes she said it was 'bloody awful' to which their father would say 'language' and Ava would reply 'you say it.' This sort of comment usually made their dad go rigid and Ava would tell him not to get 'stressed out' which would make him much more stressed out.

At times like this, Jake tried to ease the situation with a song. His favourite was The Wheels on the Bus because Miss Cunning sang him that one and Jake loved Miss Cunning because her voice was the colour of bananas and Jake loved bananas. But Jake's singing didn't produce the banana hue Miss Cunning's did so it was good when his dad brought his knotted face level with Jake's and smiled and joined in. Jake's dad's voice was woody and made Jake's tummy warm and full. Sometimes, though, Jake's dad wouldn't join Jake singing The Wheels on the Bus but would leave the room. On one occasion he'd stormed out of the house and was gone a whole day and night. When that had happened, Jake felt the upset flood down his chin and chest and along his legs to his feet and Ava (who was sometimes as quick as a cat and sometimes too angry with either their mum or dad or even Jake) had – thud – been given Jake's upset hard on her calf.

Ava's upset poured out of her hands, her feet, her mouth, her hair; it spread from her like a storm cloud, in all directions, including Jake's. She'd showered Jake with hailstones and her upset had hurt him like the stones had hurt him upside-down when only a moment before he'd been a Hardy Teenager racing his bike to school.

Much worse than Ava's upset, though, worse even than when she'd lashed out at him that she 'wished he'd died' that day, worse than when she'd yelled at their parents that they loved '*stupid* Jake' more than her, was Ava's grief.

Ava's 'grieving' was there in the bluish smudge under her mousy-coloured eyes. He'd heard it in the croak of her voice and the silence of her drums. He'd felt it in the lightness of her touch. Jake didn't know what it was until he heard his mother on the phone: 'The school counsellor told me she thinks Ava's… *behaviour* is because she's grieving for Jake…'

Jake had hated Ava's grief. It was shiny and black and it spiked him and he'd wanted to crawl far away from it, from Ava. Because Jake knew people grieved for the dead, the way Gary with his indigo blue drill said he missed his mother, who'd had cancer; the way Jake's grandpa got lost sometimes, thinking of Jake's grandma. But Jake knew he was not dead.

He remembered, upside-down, when the breath was forced from his lungs. He remembered the effort to force the breath back in. Ava's 'grieving' had told Jake he was a Ghost Boy.

Being a Ghost Boy was like being half-alive. People whispered around him, about him: 'What a tragedy,' they'd hiss. They strained to avoid his questioning eyes or instead shouted empty encouragement: 'GOOD LAD, KEEP FIGHTING.' They cried over 'poor Jakey' and said how they missed him, even though he was there, just there, sitting, listening.

Lately at least, Ava was freer of shadow. She played the drums and shared with Jake the delicious marshmallow beats.

Ava drew the sitting room curtains and then turned on Jake's special ceiling light. Jake's special light changed from blue to violet to red to yellow and then flashed on-off, on-off and then dimmed and then brightened.

As Jake and Ava watched the light, Ava told Jake about her day, which seemed to Jake to involve a lot of things Ava found 'so dull' because Ava's school, which had once been Jake's school when he was a Hardy Teenager, was 'stupid' – not like Jake's school which had Miss Cunning and the music room and trips to the farm.

When their mother came in she said something in a soft way to Ava which Ava liked because she stayed in the sitting room when often she'd leave to go to her room to be 'alone.' Their mother brought her face level with Jake's and she told him that the bruise on her leg was the worst yet and that she was sorry not to have vacuumed before when Jake was at school but that she'd been at work all day and had not had time to tidy up the spilt breakfast cereal from that morning and could he please not kick her.

Jake gave her his best smile which always made her smile and then she blew a raspberry on his cheek which always made him laugh and laughter to Jake looked like confetti falling.

He squeezed the ball, because laughter made him strong. The colour of Ava's sigh joined the baked bean tune. Jake closed his eyes and watched the colours, noises far removed from the sky-splitting crack of the car which had hit the back wheel of his Hardy Teenager racing bike and spun him upside-down only fifteen months ago.

Jake's dad's face was suddenly level with Jake's and he said: 'Hey Jakey.' Jake said hey dad in his special way that his dad had quickly understood and then his mum and then Ava and now Miss Cunning. Not many others understood Jake, not even grandpa whose eyes watered when he looked at Jake even when Jake sang The Wheels on the Bus or was telling him happy things like marshmallow beats.

Not that anyone really understood about the coloured sounds. Sometimes he thought Ava understood. Once, as they both listened to the heavy drumbeat of The White Stripes on the iPod, Ava had left him for just a minute then had come back with a bag of marshmallows – actual soft, pinky white ones. She'd put one in Jake's mouth and as the sweetness melted and he listened to Seven Nations Army, Jake Bennett thought he'd never in his life been so happy.

Elinor Nash has been painting and writing for thirty years, a passion that began with illustrated stories of her toys and cat. After she finished a PGCE in Primary Teaching, she kept on drawing but left the writing alone until five years ago when she had an idea to write a novel.

Under the name Ele Nash, Elinor exhibits paintings in and around her home city of Bath. She uses newspapers, zips, buttons, bra-straps – anything that's been discarded. She writes fiction in much the same way, piecing together ideas and experiences. Elinor is a member of the Golden Egg Academy, where Imogen Cooper, Editor at Chicken House Publishers, is advising her on her first novel, *The Lemon Sliced Moon*.

Elinor only began writing short stories two years ago after discovering the amazing Bath Writing Events group where she was inspired to try competitions. The Bath Short Story Award is the first competition she's won, which she describes as 'a shocking and lovely confidence boost!'

When Elinor's not knuckle deep in collage paper or print outs of stories, she tends to her three beautiful children, three demanding cats, one squeaky guinea pig and one very patient husband. Elinor's writing website: www.writinglark.weebly.com

Lucy Luck commented:

'A strong and impressive voice, beautifully controlled. A young boy disabled in a bike accident is real and vivid on the page, and we see how the world has changed for him and for those around him through the marshmallow and baked bean sounds of the everyday. Top marks.'

SECOND PRIZE
KIT DE WAAL

The Beautiful Thing

I met my father in 1969 when I was ten, I don't mean we were estranged; he lived with us, I saw him every day. But one evening, at the kitchen table, while he polished his heavy winter boots, he started talking about coming to England and the day he got off the boat and I saw then he had a life that stretched back before I was born. So that's how I met him and this is what he told me.

My father and Judas were sitting in the bar on Moon Street, a long airless room, shuttered from the heat. My father drained his warm, half-share of beer and pushed the glass away.

'We going then Judas? You sure?'

Judas smiled.

My father wanted someone keen for adventure and for the long trip to England so he shook hands with Judas and went his way. They would stick together, make a go of it, send money back and one day, come home themselves with cash in their pockets and a tale to tell. There was three weeks to wait before the ship sailed and time enough to see if Judas would change his mind like he'd changed it so many times, when they were children, when they climbed into the sweet shop, grabbed what they could, pledged their silence and ran. But Judas told. They were beaten and disgraced, the uneaten sweets restored to the shop. And Judas earned his name. By the time he was twenty-eight his treachery was almost forgotten.

My father had left Antigua before. He was nineteen when he took the boat to Florida to cut sugar cane in The Glades for five dollars a day. He picked oranges in Pahokee, living in a shack with twenty other men and then worked his way slowly north through the plantation fields of Georgia and Alabama where a black man took his life in his hands every time he stepped on the street. He laboured in the saw mills and lumber yards of The Carolinas, heaving and hauling something or other all the way to New York City where he felt his first winter.

'New York was bright like a summer's day,' he said, 'but cold like ice water.'

He was a warehouse hand in a grain store, loading unwieldy bags of rice and corn in East Flatbush.

'Them bags was heavy as a dead man. You had to wear gloves or the cloth would tear the skin of your palms. Disease would get in and before you know it, you can't work and that is worse than sickness. If you are sick, it only last a few days. Anyway, you take your two hands like this and you grab the sack like you're a caveman and you just found a wife.'

He threw the wife over his shoulder.

'Now you have to make a pile over in the corner.'

He pointed to the far side of the kitchen and stumbled towards it and threw the invisible sack down.

'By the afternoon, all you want is your bed. All you want is to stop. All you want is the easy job the white man gets. But you're not white and you have your cavewoman on your shoulder, and you have a mother in Antigua with diabetes. So you make your pile grow, hour after hour you make it grow and to make the time pass you start racing yourself. Then you race the clock, then you race the man next to you.

'It's a game now and you find a little fun in it and you're shouting at each other and people are running bets. "Lofty to win," they say because I'm gone six foot by now. The other guy is from Dominica where they grow small but tough. It's not easy but I'm in front and everyone's watching, cheering. Then the foreman comes over, a Puerto Rican who thinks he's better than us. He's a black man still, but he's light skinned and we are dark. Anyway, he tells us to stop. There's noise now. My blood is hot, the sweat is on my back. My sacks are high but the Dominican's sacks are wide and this race means everything to me. It means I'm good for something and I can come out on top. I can't stop. I can't.

'The white boss comes. Now it's different. He takes his time, walks slow, everything stops. The man comes right up to me and stands so close I feel the heat from his cigar. He shakes his head and calls me jiggaboo.

'Jiggaboo,' he says 'we don't need boys that can't take orders. I thought you would have known how to take orders, jiggaboo. Thought it would be in your blood.'

My father twisted his feet into his boots and stood up. The laces trailed on the kitchen floor as he walked to the stove. He took two cups from the shelf and made cocoa for us both, three sugars for me, four for himself. If I knew then that the sugar would kill him, I might have said something but I was ten years old and I was angry with the white man and wanted my father to box him down.

But instead he cut us each a slice of fruit cake and ate his slowly with his eyes closed.

'Did you fight him, Dad?

'No,' he said after a while. 'He sacked me. Told me to get out. Right there, in front of the others. Gave me half an hour to leave. I picked up my money, just a few dollars. In a week I was back home sitting on that stool in Moon Street making plans with Judas.'

Some of this I'd heard before; my father, twenty days on the ship, getting colder and colder, with bad food and good company, marking time on a bed as narrow as a prison bunk waiting to see the Motherland.

'We didn't think of ourselves as foreigners. She was our Queen too. You believed those things then. You believed you belonged somewhere. But then again, we heard the stories. Black people being called names, getting spat on, things like that. We heard someone got attacked and robbed in London town but we knew him as a drinker so thought it must have been a bar room fight. We hoped. We had to hope. Well, anyway when we are coming in to dock, me and Judas get dressed up in our best clothes. You have to make a good impression.'

My father stood up.

'First,' he said, 'a good trilby, pulled down at the front, like so. Next, an overcoat, brand new, heavy, gabardine.'

He smoothed down the lapels, undid the imaginary belt and showed me inside.

'Now,' he said 'my suit,' and the light came into his eyes. 'When you are tall, and you will be tall, nothing can beat a good suit. It was dark grey, mohair and wool. And then a white cotton shirt and a red tie in a Windsor knot.'

My father turned around so I could admire his outfit. He winked.

'I was slender then so you have to use your imagination.'

He looked down at his feet.

'I was wearing spats. I saved up for months. Spats was all the fashion in America. Black shoes with a white leather front, buttons up the side. Lovely.'

He bent down and tied his bootlaces.

'Boat after boat was arriving from the West Indies, from Jamaica, Barbados, St. Lucia. I was just one more black man standing on the dock looking for work. But we had an address in Manchester for a job and a room and there were other men going the same way, a couple of women as well. Good looking women.'

He winked again.

'We walked off the boat in a big group, all together, and they showed us into a Customs room. We had our passports ready, British passports.'

He made a noise with his tongue against his teeth, a long hiss. I knew what it meant.

'We were coloureds to them. We were blackies. And they asked us a whole lot of questions about where we were going and how much money we brought and things like that. Eventually we got out on to the street. People were staring at us. Stopping and pointing, white men in gangs looking at me and Judas and the rest of us. We heard more names, worse ones, "nigger", "monkey", "wog". We had to get to the bus station quickly, we had to get away. So we started walking. I didn't like it. At least in America there were black men on the street, you didn't stand out so much. But here? And then, the more I looked, the more I noticed something. Nobody had on spats.'

He looked down at his feet.

'All the English men had on black shoes or black boots, plain black, lace up. Like these.'

He shook his head and sighed.

'And there is me in my ten dollar spats. I looked different. I looked wrong. I stopped walking. I can't do it. I can't go all the way to Manchester looking like this. I can't change the colour of my skin but I can change my shoes.'

He pointed in the distance.

'There it was, a shoe shop. I say to Judas, 'Come Judas. Come with me into that shop so I can buy a new pair of shoes.'

'The others kept going and Judas looked at me. He looked at the little shoe shop and the white men standing on the corner and he shook his head. "No, Lofty. I'm staying with the others," he said. He walked away. Turned the corner. Gone. I was on my own.'

I pictured Judas, the fat man with the easy smile who came to our house every Christmas, played dominoes with my father, balanced his glass of rum on the arm of the chair.

'What happened, Dad?' I said, raging inside.

'I let him go. Judas, Judas he doesn't change, even now. Anyway, I walked into the shop. There was an old man and a woman, must have been his wife and some customers. "Yes?" said the man. I pointed at the black shoes in the window and told him I needed a pair in a size 10. Everyone was looking at me. I didn't even put down my case and there was no price on the shoes. I was spending the money I had brought to live on. I was thinking all the time, "Get out Lofty, what you doing?" But the man brought me the shoes. "These are twelve and nine, sir," he said and pointed to a chair. I didn't know he meant the price. I thought he bought me odd sizes but I just sat down on the little chair. And then you know what happened?'

'What, Dad?'

'The woman comes over to me and she kneels down. She takes off my spats and she put on one black shoe. She laces it and then she does the same again. When she looks up at me, she is smiling. "How does that feel, sir?" she says. "Is that alright?"'

My father had his arms crossed and his head high. His eyes were closed and he was smiling.

'A white woman at my feet, treating me with respect. "Is that alright, sir?" she said. It was a beautiful thing.'

He was silent for some time. I could hear him breathing.

'What happened to the spats, Dad? Have you still got them?'

'No, no,' he said. 'I left them with the lady. She collected things for the poor. We had a good conversation. She shook my hand when I left and said, "Good Luck".'

'She was nice, wasn't she, Dad?'

'Yes,' he said. 'A good woman.'

He put on his bus jacket and badge and squeezed the knot of his tie. I passed him his flask and his bag and he sighed as he put it over his shoulder. As we walked together to the front door, he shouted upstairs to tell my mother he was gone and then looked at me.

'Be good,' he said.

He shook my hand for the first time and held it a while.

'And don't be angry. If you look, you will always find a beautiful thing.'

From the doorstep I watched him go. I saw him hunch and shiver, check his watch, turn up his collar and heard above his soft whistle, the ringing of his boot-tips on the wet English street.

Kit de Waal spent fifteen years in criminal and family law before becoming a writer. She writes short stories, flash fiction, and longer form prose. She is published in various anthologies (*Fish Prize 2011 & 2012; The Sea in Birmingham 2013; Final Chapters 2013*) and works as an editor of non-fiction. In 2014 she gained second place in the Costa Short Story Award with 'The Old Man & The Suit'. She is currently working on a novel.

Lucy Luck commented:

'Really strong story-telling perfectly paced and pitched. I love the father's voice, and the way we move between New York, Antigua, the shoe shop and the kitchen is beautifully handled, and the ending is extremely well-done. Very good indeed.'

THIRD PRIZE
ALEX HAMMOND

No Man's Land

He has built no man's land. There, in the dead ground at the
top of the garden, where the old conservatory once stood.
Dead ground where the ambitious Spanish factory worker
grew grapevines to make his own wine; now the factory is
closed, and the old man has gone home to Spain to lay to rest
his own ghost of Franco.

They have not lived there long, though the boy's father
has already been busy. He knocked the conservatory down as
soon as they moved in. Behind the boy's British lines, across
a river of old concrete that is the garden path, is a small, new
flowerbed. The first flush of summer flowers push through
the daisies; antirrhinum buds ready to burst into bloom, roses
splashing bloodred against the green of a privet hedge. The
boy understands the stories, and the new growth makes sense
to his gamescape; British Generals take tea under roses, and
listen on old telephones to their aides who have climbed the
flower stems to report on the day's action.

Shoots of new grass already push through the zig-zagging British lines; before play begins, the boy must carefully pull these shoots from his diorama, lest the encroach of green give lie to the game and bring slender threads of peace to his own little Western Front. In their place, he drives carefully selected twigs and branches into the earth. Studied close against the old grainy photos of the original battlefields, they now stand as sentinels; fallen miniatures of their mighty forebears, stripped by imagined shellfire and shattered by the truth the boy perceives in those photographs.

The German lines are more complicated; deep bunkers to withstand the heavy artillery of his digging stick. The cratered moonscape of the photos must be recreated, and no plastic soldier may lie without the corresponding shellhole to mark the manner of his falling. Behind the German lines, metal-red leaves of the acer shake in the soft summer breeze; it is doing well, thriving on the outskirts of the battlefield; new roots interfere with digging bunkers; already spreading and clutching the earth. His father digs deep in planting. Buddleia too, growing behind the German lines, robbing the boy of the perfect colour balance for Goodies and Baddies.

The boy has a problem. It is his first day of the Somme, and today he carefully digs Lochnagar Crater in the German lines. But it won't hold water. It must hold water. There must be mud, because without mud it's not the Somme. He fills the crater and the thirsty Hampshire earth drinks it up greedily; the sun in its brilliance robs what remains of the boy's constructed hell. He has been filling the crater for fifteen minutes. There is no thick, clay-like, drowning mud to cling to the boots and square bases of his toy soldiers. It is not right. Time to get help.

The shade blinkers him after the brightness of the late-morning sun. 'Dad?' he calls.

'Yeah?

'Dad I need help.'

'You okay?'

'Yeah. I need to stop my crater from draining away.'

'What?'

'Come look, I'll show you.'

'I'm a little busy right now.'

'Come on. It'll only take a minute.'

There is the audible sigh adults make when they get out of a chair, when anything is asked of them.

His dad appears in old jeans and a paint-spattered sweater. 'What's up mate?

'Come on, I'll show you.'

The boy takes the lead, his dad follows. They skirt the battlefield. The boy points to Lochnagar Crater. 'It won't stay full.'

'You sure you don't want to build Mummy's armoured car? I've unpacked the box with your lego in.'

'Yes, I want to build Mum's armoured car. But not now. Lego is for when it's dark outside.'

'So what are you playing now?'

'Somme.'

'Right.'

Dad crouches down, avoids leaving a boot-print on the carefully constructed slaughterhouse. 'What you need,' he says, 'is a bowl. Something to store the water in so the earth doesn't drink it all up.'

'Will that make it muddy?'

'Why do you want it muddy?'

'Because that's what happened.'

'On the Somme?'

'Yes.'

'There wasn't any mud on the first day of the Somme.'

'There is in mine.'

Dad chuckles. 'Poor Tommies.'

'It's not funny Dad. It's very sad and serious. Thousands and thousands of men were killed.' The boy straightens up. 'So how do I get mud?'

Dad stands up and wanders down to the bottom of the

shed. The boy follows like a shadow, watches while Dad braves giant shed-dwelling spiders and other creepy-crawlies and comes back with the round plastic base of a flower-pot. 'Bury this in your crater, and fill it with water. It'll stop the water draining away.'

'And then I'll get the mud?'

'If you mix some of the soil in with the water, it'll make you a mud bath that's not going anywhere fast.'

'Thanks Dad.'

'That's alright mate. Just don't get any mud in the house.'

Dad returns upstairs. He keeps unpacking. Mum is tired, she drove all morning, and is sleeping fitfully; he looks at her. There it is again. She doesn't sleep properly, not since she got back. He thinks of his son making mud and wonders if in a hundred years, some father will help his son recreate the dust that choked his wife while she plugged wounds in Afghanistan. He can almost hear it: 'Dad,' says the voice, 'Dad, how do I get snow to stay on top of the mountains?'

She carefully walks the garden in bare feet. She can smell the dew-damp earth where her son has dug a battlefield. He left his soldiers out overnight: 'Soldiers sleep outdoors, don't they Mum?'

She looks at the craters and can hear his soft childish lips, cheeks puffed out, saliva flying, quietly making the sound of explosions. The bigger the explosion, the softer he makes the sound; he knows, somehow, that his voice cannot be that horrible, that sudden. He whispers the worst of it.

She flicks her cigarette ash and watches the smoke drift over the battlefield. Smoke. That's what the craters are missing; what those soldiers poised in the trenches, waiting for her son to come and call them out for a dawn attack, are missing. There would be smoke. There is smoke. Pain. Noise. Stink. A greenish-yellow shape huddles in a shellhole. Standing, the toy soldier would be looking forward, feet braced fore and aft, leaning into the recoil from his weapon.

But he lies on his back, the muzzle of his little plastic gun poking from the edge of the shellhole. She looks down at him and then back at the lines her son has dug. One of those carefully lined up toy soldiers will have to go and get him; a plastic soldier will run out into the imagined hail of imagined bullets and try to save the plastic toy life lying yellow in the shellhole. She can't see any medics in there. She doesn't think they mould medics in the 99p toy soldier sets. Why would they? Plastic doesn't bleed.

She finishes her cigarette, blows the last smoke towards the wounded plastic man in the stick-dug shellhole. Her boy, her son, has built this very well; this is just like those pictures he was showing them in the hotel on the drive down here, to the new house. She wants to tell him that.

She can't. She can't because he has done it so well she wants to crawl across that earth and with fingertips check that the plastic man in the shellhole is alive, is okay, is not crying out for help, a drink. She can't do that because this no man's land of her boy's is too right. His little wounded soldier is too perfectly where a wounded soldier would be, would crawl if he could, for her to praise him for it.

She steps back on the concrete path, skirting the battlefield, heading back towards the house, and pauses to fill up the watering can. She waters the summer flowers, returning to the battlefield, stepping around it. She waters the acer, the buddleia. There is some water left in the can. She scoops some dried mud from a plastic tray dug into the ground, wipes it clean with her fingers. She tucks it back into the crater and fills it with clean water. The toy soldiers, after the attack to come, will at least have something clean to drink. She can do that for them.

She goes back inside and shuts the door. It's too early. She won't go back to bed though. She won't go back to sleep.

Alex Hammond studied Creative Writing at UEA and at Lancaster University and is due to begin a PhD at Southampton University in October 2014. He previously wrote for the now defunct *Taste of the Wight* magazine and has worked in publishing and digital marketing. He is a musician, playing percussion in the blues and skiffle band The Dodge Brothers. His fiction has been published in the university anthologies *Enormous Rooms* (University of Utah, 2006) and *Workshop* (University of East Anglia, 2007). He is currently working on his first novel about returning veterans and a collection of short stories drawing on his experiences as a Special Constable in the Metropolitan Police Service.

Lucy Luck commented:

'The tone of the piece is impressive and I particularly liked the shift of PoV and the way this moment in time (an afternoon, an evening) is used to such effect to highlight the noise and trauma of a war zone. Characterisation strong, ending very strong.'

LOCAL PRIZE & COMMENDED
ANNE CORLETT

The Language of Birds

It's a strange thing, this slow slipping-away of self.

It's as though my sole function is a long, drawn-out disintegration of which I'm barely aware, until I have cause to go rootling in some disused corner of my mind. That's when I find the gaps, the blocked-off segments of memory, the little consortia of synapses that have quietly shut up shop and drifted away, without a word of farewell.

My life has no grain or texture. Yesterday fades swiftly into uncertainty. Last week is a myth, a fairytale I only half-believe.

My world is shrinking, contracting to this single room. Not even that. To this chair, the blanket on my lap, and the well-worn cushion at the small of my back. No wonder that there's little that can hold my attention for more than a moment or two.

It's only the old memories that have any strength.

And the birds.

It was the last thing Henry did for me. Clawing back

a brief, late-blooming strength from the tight grasp of his illness, he hung the feeders all around the windows, so that whichever way I turned my head, I'd see them.

They come every day, clockwork-regular, their constant presence freeing me from the fear of forgetting.

I once read a story about a man who wanted to live forever, and was given that life for the time it took a bird to peck away a mountain.

Death is always portrayed with a scythe, a bearer of swift oblivion. But I think death comes for the old with a chisel, a file, a hard little beak, wearing us away to a nub.

The robins are here. They always arrive simultaneously, from opposite ends of the garden, launching into their usual territorial squabblings, scrapping and flapping at one another, to mark out *this is mine*.

They remind me of my boys. The way they arrived in this world together, already bawling and flailing at one another, their whole childhood spent in a state of boisterous strife, which continued well into adulthood. It took half a lifetime before they found a way of fitting together, without their sharp corners and rough edges colliding in a shower of sparks.

I miss their visits. I miss the way they used to knock on the door, a confident tattoo that seemed to shout 'I'm here! Are you glad I'm here?'

They still come, of course.

When they can.

But their visits seem to slip away, and I find myself turning petulant, as though it's their fault that I can't hold onto the memories for more than a day or so.

But I remember when they were children.

I remember how I hoarded them, gloated over them, as proof that I had won out against death. They always smiled more brightly for me than for anyone else, their arms reaching for me in a perpetual demand to be *up up up*. I never refused them, clutching them to me, their warmth forcing away the chill that always seemed to be whispering at the back of my neck, as though the winters of years ago were still following me.

A couple of blue-tits are dangling from the suet balls. They're ridiculously fragile things. Just little scraps of bright feather and hollow bone. They kept hurling themselves at the window during that long, cold winter before Henry began to fade. He'd find them, still and frozen, and try to hide the little corpses from me, as though I'd never seen death.

But then I never told him how well acquainted we were, death and I.

It's strange how the memories rise at odd, disconnected moments.

Like when I was birthing the boys. I was somewhere beyond myself, racked and retching with the force of something fundamental and terrifying, and the past saw its chance and swept in.

It wasn't a good birth. Not as bad as some I'd seen, but pretty bad, nonetheless. At the peak of it, I was sure I was labouring in a grave, with a waiting shroud, not a swaddle.

We give birth astride a grave.

I remember when that was true, when I saw women labouring among corpses, with just the chill and press of an overcrowded grave at the end of it all.

Childbirth is a uniquely female debasement. I hated the exposure of my hidden places. I suppose I'd seen too much in the way of women's flesh.

In the camp, I was surrounded by the erosion and death of women. Female suffering is a secret thing, all mixed up with shame and guilt. We bleed, deep down in our bodies, even when we're dying. We can be forced and broken from within. When the women's hair was taken, even their bald skulls became an obscenity, all those bumps and contours revealed, as unnatural as bone through cracked flesh.

I only worked in the processing sheds for a short while, but for years afterwards I used to imagine I could feel stray hairs on my hands, a shadow-touch that made me flail at my skin. I don't know why it was the hair that stayed with me, more than all the other female indignities; those bundles of stained rags, huddling amongst the discarded clothing; or the sight of those chosen few, returning from behind the barracks, hunched and huddled, a guiding male hand on their backs in a parody of chivalry.

I once walked in on one of the guards with a woman. He looked at me. *Do you mind,* he said, perfectly polite. *We're a little busy.*

We.

The lies we tell ourselves.

Those women were at my side through my own births, a silent host of witness, while I cried and floundered and begged for an ending, and it was their cold hands in mine, as I slipped into the heavy darkness which preceded my motherhood.

With a flash of bright feathers outside the window, the goldfinches arrive in untidy formation.

They make me smile, these tiny clowns of the bird world, so pointlessly gaudy, so puffed-up with their own importance.

They'll only deign to eat niger seed. If it runs out, they form themselves into a garish flock of accusation, settling briefly to glare in at me, before taking off again, winding themselves into a frenzy of indignant, thwarted greed.

Nijer seed, they spell it now, apparently. The lady at the garden centre told me, blushing at the thought, that people kept mispronouncing it.

The finches remind me of the girls in town, strutting, straight-legged, arms linked, painted and shrill, their voices vying in a constant stream of wanting-it-all.

Even in the camp, the young girls chattered, as though words were life.

There was one who kept talking in the line, all the way in through the door. Even as the engines clanged and clanked into life, I could still hear her talking, although I did not understand the words. I heard her voice right up to the moment that it was engulfed by that great, multi-throated wail that I'd heard so many times, it had engraved itself into the inside of my skull.

In the field beyond the garden, the grass is silver-white with dandelion clocks. Some day soon, I'll wake and they'll be gone, the field green again. I probably won't remember that they were ever there. There'll be a faint niggle of difference, and I'll worry over it, like a loose tooth, but the dandelions will be gone, another little corner of myself lost to eternity.

There are larks wheeling in the clear sky above the field.

They're always treated as sacred, the larks, like little scraps of heaven. But, to me, they always seem like fallen angels, singing gaily that I am a liar.

They always sang above the camp. Even as the fires burned and the women died, the larks kept singing, twisting themselves higher and higher into the sky, as though to storm heaven with their song. Dancing above the gas chambers, singing as though they loved us.

They were singing the day I met Henry.

The camps were falling apart, as the great German war-machine broke down before the advance of the allies.

I was working in the big house by then, and I stood at the fence, watching the world unravelling. One of the guards, an older woman, took me aside.

I don't know why. I'd never seen a single act of kindness fall from her hands before.

'You say you were always a house-servant,' she said. 'You say you were never in the camp. You never tell. Never tell them what you were.'

Her tone was harsh, accusatory, and I was surprised to find a faint flicker of answering anger, licking up inside of me. I'd thought that all emotions of that kind had burned down into ashes long ago.

'I had no choice,' I said 'They'd have killed me too.'

She laughed, a hard death-rattle of a sound. 'You had a choice,' she said.

I watched her walk away, stiff-backed and slow, and then I went back to the house and waited, sitting silently at the kitchen table with another woman, another kapo. I didn't know her name, and we did not meet each other's eyes, afraid, I suppose, of what we might see mirrored there.

There was a clatter of boots from overhead. Raised voices, the language unfamiliar.

We waited. Doors banged. The feet moved across the floor, our eyes tracking their unseen progress.

Then the kitchen door, and the rhythmical creak of the stairs, as someone descended.

The man was young, fair-haired, like my own people, but in the uniform of a British officer.

His looked at the two of us, his eyes flickering across our uniforms, and then he smiled, reassuringly.

'Gefangene? Prisoners?'

We nodded.

'You were in the camp?' His eyes were gentle as he asked the question, repeating it in broken German.

I looked at the other woman for the first time. Her face was expressionless.

I turned back to the young officer and shook my head.

'No. Just here. In the house. They told us to work here.'

The other woman said nothing, her silence colluding with my deception, wrapping us round in a muffling layer of denial.

The young man sat down at the table. He told us his name was Henry.

The other woman made some coffee, using the Kommandant's best cups.

Our conversation was patched together from my meagre

supply of English, and his barely more fluent German, but when he spoke of the camps, I saw the flash of anger in his eyes, and my chest tightened with apprehension.

I felt around for something to say, trying to imagine what I would be asking him, if I had never set foot beyond the Kommandant's garden.

When I found the lie, so close to hand that it seemed like forgiveness, I seized it with relief, slipping into her skin, that other woman, that other me, who didn't know what shape betrayal made, right down in the cold space at the bottom of your lungs.

'Are they alright?' I asked him. 'The others. What we heard about that place, is it true?'

The other kapo got up from the table and crossed to the kitchen sink, walking carefully, precisely, as though the air around her might break with one incautious movement.

I watched her go, and then turned back to look at Henry.

Something moved in the shadows behind his eyes, but he found a smile for me. 'It's fine,' he lied. 'Don't worry about it. You're safe now.'

And so we set the language of our lives together.

Wherever I go, I hear the larks singing.

I wake to the sound of it. I hear it vibrating in my skull-bones as I doze in my chair, and it lulls me into a dream-racked sleep by night. It's as though the falling-away of the here-and-now is leaving me husked and hollow, just an empty space in which the larks, and the old memories, sing.

I shift the blanket over my knees. I'm suddenly cold. There's something not right.

It takes me a moment to realise what it is.

It's silence.

The birds have fallen quiet, their heads quirked, as though listening for something.

When the knock comes in a hard, staccato clatter, it's as though I've been waiting for it forever.

I've learnt so many languages. The language of my homeland. The language of my husband. The language of birds. The language of lies.

And now I realise that doors have a language too. Just as I always knew which of my children was knocking, I know what lies behind my door. I don't know what face it wears, but I know its purpose.

My chest tightens. I wonder if this is the beginning of the way in which I will die, my breath catching and dwindling inside my chest.

The birds have averted their eyes from me now, as though unwilling to stand witness to this reckoning.

The knock comes again. And then, across seven decades, a thousand miles, the larks launch into a final, triumphant trill.

And then silence.

At last.

Anne Corlett spent thirteen years as a criminal lawyer. She is still unsure how this happened, given a firm intention to work in publishing, two linguistic degrees and a stint as an etymologist. She has now returned to writing and has completed two novels, for which she is represented by the Richford Becklow Agency.

She also writes non-fiction for magazines. About eighteen months ago, concerned about her apparent inability to tell a story in fewer than 140,000 words, she decided to give short fiction a try. She has been longlisted and shortlisted for various prizes, including Bath, Mslexia, Fish, Writers' Forum, Words with Jam and New Writer. She was third in the 2013 Bristol Prize and recently won the HE Bates Prize.

She lives near Bath with her partner and two small children. This is probably a bad idea, since she is originally from Tyneside and cannot, according to her increasingly Bristolian four-year old, pronounce 'Bath' properly. She occasionally rants at http://consummatechaosblog.blogspot. co.uk/ and reads regularly at the Story Friday events in Bath — www.awordinyourear.org.uk

Lucy Luck commented:

'Very good opening, very good voice, the scene is set impressively and I like the way the story of the narrator's life and lie are unveiled, and how we come to understand that the knowledge of this lie will go when her memory goes – that she has got away with it. Made me feel uncomfortable that I sympathised with the narrator when I realised how she has managed to live around a secret this psychologically profound. Thought-provoking, there's a lot beneath the words.'

COMMENDED
LISA HARDING

It's a Girl

Vilmos makes me do it. He says I will earn more money, that
the people here would feed an animal before they would feed
one of us. I listen to him, like my bata listens to him, since
she became his wife. He tells me to put the small dog on my
lap and to pat it. I do not want to touch it. He tells me I must.
He tells me to look down if a man comes near me. Never
go anywhere with a man from this country – they are not to
be trusted, he says. He tells me to look sad and smile. I am
sixteen and I am married to Sabin. He is Vilmos' cousin and
he is old. He chews gum, he says it keeps him warm.

The creature cleans itself with its tongue. It has such a
bad smell in its mouth. Sabin went to a shop this morning and
bought a coat for it, because so many people were giving out
that the thing was cold. It is a red coat with fur on its edges
and a little boy said to his mother today: 'Oh look Mama, it is
Santa's little helper.'

My little boy Luca is sixteen months now. He does not

have a coat with fur. Yesterday when I got home his nappy was full and he had something yellow in his eyes. Vilmos tells me if I bring in enough money I can spend time with him one day a week and I won't be driven here when it is still dark and picked up when it is past night. My hips hurt from the cold concrete and wet air. Luca clings to me tightly when I am at home. He was happier with me out here than he is in that house where no natural light gets through. Vilmos tells me it is not safe to have my baby on the streets. The people in the blue suits won't allow it. I used to love to snuggle into him and smell his beautiful baby smell. He could drink milk from me when he wanted. The animal tries to nuzzle its nose into my neck. I am sure it is hungry but I cannot think of that when I think that my boy is hungry. It puts its mouth in my pocket. I ate a meat sandwich at McDonalds today and kept some in a napkin for baby for later.

'What's her name?' a woman with blonde hair asks. She is beautiful when I see her first. Her eyes are light blue and seem to have water floating in them. I do not know what she means. Who is her? 'The puppy...what's her name?' I shrug. How does she know it is a girl. A name? It has a tail that belongs to a rat, and ears that move by themselves. It is covered in hair.

'She's lovely,' the woman says.

I look at her in that pleading way that my bata taught me, with the palms of my hands facing skywards and say, 'Please, please, money for the puppy.' I know that 'Please help, I am hungry,' does not work.

'If I give you money would you really buy the puppy food?' the blonde woman says.

'Yes mam, please mam, puppy hungry,' I say.

'You certainly don't look hungry,' she says.

I am carrying another baby inside of me. I eat meat sandwiches every day. I wear five layers of clothing. My face is puffy. I am not pretty and I tell Vilmos this. 'They do not give me money because I am not pretty.'

'They will give you money for the puppy,' he says. He is wrong. Most of them, they do not look at me, or if they do, they stop, like this woman, they touch the animal on the head and rub its back, and tell me it is starving. Sometimes they get angry and say that it is a disgrace, that I am a disgrace. I understand that word. I want to say I have to do this, but I know that Sabin is never very far away, and it would get back to Vilmos and that would be bad for me, for Luca, for the baby in my belly, and my bata, so I say, 'Please, money for the puppy.'

'I will go and get that puppy food,' the woman says, 'and I will make sure it eats it here on the street.'

'McDonalds?' I ask.

The woman brings her face close to mine and it does not look at all beautiful close up. There is a layer of orange dust on her face that catches in the tiny lines around her eyes, and the deep ridge above her nose. Her lips are painted dark pink and they are made to look wider than they are. The lashes on the outside of her eyes are covered in black sticky stuff, some of which has fallen on to her cheeks below. I see that at the top of her blonde hair, where it comes out of her head, there is black.

I do not know what she means by bringing her face so close to mine, but I know it is not friendly. I think she thinks there is something bad about how I look. I do not understand all of what the people do or say here. I did not go to school. Vilmos told my bata that it is not good for a child to grow up speaking a language her mother does not understand. My bata listened, and none of the other children he gave her go to school either. My friend Maria goes and she says it is better than being on the streets.

My legs are hurting and I get up to walk around. I hold the wriggling creature tight. The woman stares at me, like I was something she had never seen before.

'Do you ever walk the poor little mite?' she says.

I shake my head. 'No understand. Puppy hungry, please

help.'

'Oh I'll help alright.' Her cheeks become red and the water in her eyes is coming to the surface.

She walks away and I see her talking to the Garda-man. Her voice is loud. He is shaking his head at her. Vilmos knows there is nothing they can do when it is an animal, but when it is a child they can take it away and take all your money from you. I am needing to go to the toilet. I look around me and I do not see Sabin. He is usually never very far away. I walk back to McDonalds. They let me use the toilet if they are too busy to see me. One day, a boy, about my age, would not let me in. He told me I should get my stinking ass on a plane back to my stinking country. I do not remember my country. I do not know how my bata and I came to be here, where the sun does not show itself often, and when it does it is watery and it is not warm. I think I remember what warm feels like. My bata tells me we came in on the air, and points to a machine that flies through the clouds. I wish I could remember being above the low, grey sky that is almost always crying cold tears.

I go to McDonalds and I hope that Sabin is following me, even though he will be angry as I have already had my lunch and he might think I am going to buy more food. I cannot see him. I put the creature down on the pavement and it sniffs and licks the concrete like it will find something to eat there. I have a piece of rope and I start to tie it to a metal-stand which has bicycles locked to it, when I stop. I cannot do this. It might be taken and I would be in trouble, which would mean my bata, my baby and Luca would be in trouble too. I clench the muscles inside of me and feel the pressure of the baby pressing down on me. I have to hold it, and although it is getting harder as the baby is getting bigger, I tell myself that after ten minutes the worst of it will be over. As I bend to untie the animal I see the blonde woman coming towards me.

'Enjoy your McDonalds?' she says. She gets down on the ground and opens a can of dark brown food for the dog and she starts to feed it with a plastic fork. 'Want some?' the woman asks me. I understand her question and I shake my head. 'That shit in there is the same shit that's in here,' the woman says, pointing first at McDonalds and then at the can. The dog is making sucking sounds.

When it is finished – it cannot eat very much – the woman looks at me and says 'How much?'

I say I do not understand, although I do. I turn my palms up.

'Oh no, please don't start your whining,' the woman says, and she presses fifty euros in to my palm. I wonder can I put it in my pocket. I wonder would I get away with not telling Vilmos about this when I see Sabin looking at me sideways, from behind a lamp post. So, he is there after all. He shakes his head at me. I shake my head at the woman.

'It's for the puppy,' says the blonde woman.

I shake my head again and the woman picks the dog up off the street and runs away. Sabin runs after her calling, 'Thief, thief.'

The woman shouts over her shoulder, 'You people.' She is stopped by the man in the blue suit and Sabin tells the man that the woman is a thief. He knows this word and repeats it over and over. The Garda-man tells the woman to give the dog back to the man. It does not belong to her.

She starts to shout, 'Listen to me, the puppy does not belong to those scum either.' I understand what she is meaning, although I do not know all the words. She asks the man to ask Sabin for papers for the puppy. The man tells the woman to "calm down," which makes her scream even louder.

'You know they do not feed them...only alcohol... they break their necks...and dump them?' She tries to speak through the crying. I think she thinks about the animal the way I do about my Luca. I wish that Sabin had let me take the fifty euros and we could have gone home early to my boy.

I look at my stomach, which is round and full with baby

and water. The worst of it is not over yet. Then I look at the woman and see that her stomach is empty and that she has no ring on her finger, which in this country means she is not married. She is getting old. I would like to let her have the baby dog to keep her company.

The Garda-man returns the dog to Sabin and says, 'Look after the little fella now, won't you son?' and the woman says, 'It's a girl, it's a little girl.'

Lisa Harding completed an MPhil in creative writing at
Trinity College Dublin in September 2013. Her short story
'Counting Down' was a winner in the inaugural Doolin
writers' prize 2013. This summer she has been shortlisted for
Doolin, Cuirt, Listowel and the Bath Short Story awards. A
story 'Call Me Moo' is to be published in the autumn issue of
The Dublin Review.

Playwriting credits include *Starving* at Theatre503, *And
All Because* at Battersea Arts Centre (as part of an emerging
writers festival: Connect Four) and *Playground* at the Project
Theatre Dublin. She is currently working on a new play
Pedigree for which she was awarded an Arts Council bursary
and a Peggy Ramsay award. As an actress she has appeared at

the Gate, the Abbey, the Lyric and on RTE, among others. Her collection of sixteen short stories *Crave* is a work in progress, alongside an embryonic novel with the working title: *The Harvesting*.

Lucy Luck commented:

'A very convincing portrayal of how it might feel to be powerless within a family group in a strange country, looking out at the world, knowing how misunderstood you have to be to survive. Nicely controlled narrative and I am impressed by how effectively I saw the world from a different perspective.'

COMMENDED
ROISÍN O'DONNELL

Under the Jasmine Tree

Virgin Maria del Carmen told me in a dream that my son was coming, so I washed my best camisole and hung it up to dry in the white heat of the *azoteya*. It's August and along the Guadalquivir they're hanging lanterns for the Triana festival. A feverish sense of expectation simmers in the streets of Seville at this time of year. Starched by the sun, my camisole dries in no time. In my lap, my pen hovers over a notebook but the blank page is frighteningly empty and the words won't come. Gold bangles tinkle nervously at my wrists and the TV chatters as I sit in its blue glare and wait.

At 4 o'clock the doorbell finally trills. My son is standing on the doorstep. He has his father's eyes. He's wearing an expensive-looking linen shirt, but the devious Andalusian heat makes a mockery of his anxious formality, and his collar is already ringed with sweat. 'Are you… Señorita Ana de Silva?' he asks in halting Spanish.

'Yes.'

'I am… at least I think I might be…?

'I know,' I tell him, and relief ripples across his face.

'You do? The office phoned you?'

I nod, thinking that it's easier to lie than to explain to my newly-found offspring that I was warned of his coming in a dream. Smiling now, the young man hands me a potted cactus, 'I'm sorry I didn't find you any flowers.'

'It's beautiful, thank-you.' I reach up to kiss him and he fumbles as foreigners often do, unfamiliar with the etiquette of Castilian kisses. This is the first time I've seen my son in thirty-three years.

I take the cactus from him and a memory blooms before me in the hot porch air. Into my open palm, Francesco placed a slender tight-lipped jasmine bud. Holding my gaze, he closed my fingers around the flower and nodded to me, as if we had settled something. I left the bud on my pillow that night, to ward off mosquitoes and scare away the *fantasmas*. Next morning, I awoke to an intoxicating perfume.

It's too hot to sit in my apartment, where the single fan is only serving to stir the treacle-like heat, so I take my son by the arm and lead him down the street towards the plastic parasol in the sky which houses Antiquarium Sevilla. Below street level, for only two euros we are able to bask in the luxurious air-conditioned cool and wander the ancient ruins, tracing arteries of forgotten streets like lines sunken into a wizened palm. We perch on the edge of a Roman settlement and my son takes out an iPad. 'I wanted to show you this,' he says, and an article flashes up on the screen under the headline

LOST SPANISH BABIES.

...*Charges are currently being investigated that thousands of Spanish infants were illegally abducted and sold for adoption over a 40-year period. What is believed to have begun as a political retaliation against leftist families during the dictatorship of General Francesco Franco evolved into a global trafficking business*

involving doctors, nurses and even nuns who colluded to…
The nun's habit was impossibly white. I watched her leathery fingers grip each other tightly as she was explaining how my baby's death had happened. Then she placed into my arms a frozen child and stood back to see my reaction. The statue of the Virgin Maria was watching too with her downcast, chipped blue eyes. The baby's soft white fingers were unresponsive to my touch. I said nothing. I knew it was not my baby.

'Are you feeling okay?' my son asks in his funny topsy-turvy Spanish, 'You don't look well.'

'I think I need some air.'

We leave the ruins and take the elevator to the café on the parasol terrace. It's baking up here and you can see the whole of Seville glistening like a mirage, with the glassy-green river snaking past the prison of Torre del Oro. My son looks down at me with concern and I catch again the resemblance to his father, who was solemn in his white robes and heavy-rimmed glasses, holding the bible for Padre Marquez and frowning intently. Mama leaned across me to whisper to Tia Ana, 'That's the new deacon. *He's from Galicia.*'

Francesco looked different, and when Padre Marquez introduced us to him at the end of mass, he spoke differently too. He didn't have the soft Sevillian lisp that I'd grown up with, where words tumble into each other without edges or corners. Each of Francesco's words was distinct, his voice clear as water and rocked with the rhythms of the sea. Behind his glasses, his dark earth-brown eyes met mine with total honesty, and for a moment we just looked at each other. When our gaze was broken, the world had changed.

My son leads me to a table at the corner of the terrace and pulls out a chair for me to sit down. 'I'm sorry,' he says, 'this must be quite a shock, me turning up like this.'

'It's okay,' I reply, 'I knew you were coming.'

We order two cold *cañas* and I study my son's slender

face. His sallow skin has been deprived of sunlight so long it has drained to the colour of old books. 'You live in England?'

'Yes,' he smiles encouragingly, 'By the way, I read *Lost Sanctuary*. Your poems are...'

'That was ten years ago,' I laugh, 'I'm surprised you found a copy.'

There passes an angel; that's what we sevillanos say when there is a sudden silence between two people like this. My son shifts in his chair, 'I have to say, you're younger than I expected... I mean you must have been very young when... when...'

'Sixteen,' I reply. My sixteenth birthday fell on the feast of Virgin Maria del Carmen, and at the parade I stood in the heat and the press of the assembled *bula*, where bodies drew closer and the drum beat steadily quickened. My skin was damp as a leaf. Strands of hair were sticking to my forehead and I could feel the bulge of my breasts in the too-tight girlish dress that Mama had made me wear. Ahead of me, the gold buttons of Javi's brass-band uniform gleamed proudly and Mama was fussing over my brother's sleek waxed hair. She didn't look back. And all the people were watching. Watching me watching Francesco, who was carrying a candle with that uncertain flame flickering in his eyes.

Smoke curled around the faces of the altar boys. Ahead, in the narrow street the statue of the Virgin emerged on a bed of white roses, her porcelain face shivering in the glow of a hundred trembling lights. Women clung to the back of the float, muttering trance-like prayers. Onlookers merged with the parade so that it was impossible to tell who was parading and who wasn't. The Virgin pushed through the cobbled streets, the crowd surging with her, carrying the drumbeat, the brass band, the shivering candlelight. Then everything was far away and I was watching it from under water, where the sound couldn't reach me.

'Ana, Ana!' I woke surrounded by people's dusty ankles, sandals, knees. 'Ana,' Francesco's breath was close to my face,

'Come, come, you've fainted Ana. Let's get you some water.'

Alone with Francesco in the sacristy, I felt the weight of what was about to happen shiver between us. The mahogany wood shone darkly. Francesco hurried over to me and put a damp cloth to my forehead. I placed my hand over his.

And on the terrace table, thirty-three years sit between myself and my son. He is relaxing with the heat and the beer, and he smiles at me, 'I never thought I'd find you... Such a long process.'

'You speak good Spanish.'

'I don't know about that,' he laughs, 'But you know the funny thing is I chose to study Spanish at uni, long before I knew... Luck, you think?'

'Fate,' I answer.

Later, when he's paying the waiter, my son opens his wallet and a picture spins out onto the table. In its well-worn creases I see my son held in the proud embrace of an older couple. 'Is that your parents?'

'Yeah, my *'parents.'* He shoves the photo into the back of his wallet. There's resentment in his voice, but it's tangled up with the type of love I've only ever known once in my life. He looks at me now and I know the question he's going to ask, 'About my dad...?'

Longing and expectation are written in my son's eyes and I have to look away from him. 'We couldn't be together. That's why they took you.' I can see the nebulas of further questions clouding my son's dark eyes, but I touch his hand gently, 'That's enough for today.'

My son walks me home, and we agree to meet at the Alcazar Gardens at seven o'clock the next evening. On parting, he forgets about the Castilian kisses and he wraps me in a hug which smells of sweat and sunlight. Francesco's robes smelt of incense, and afterwards my skin smelt of incense too. I washed it away in the shower that night; the incense smell along with the thin blood that trickled down between my thighs. *'No one will come in,'* Francesco whispered to me urgently, *'cariña... no one will know.'* But I saw the black eyes of Virgin Maria del Carmen watching me over his shoulder.

The sounds of Seville follow me into my dreams that night. Over the river, the Triana festival is in full swing and the night air is sharp with the melancholy of flamenco guitar. I first noticed my son's presence during mass, when we stood for the gospel; a tight sensation in my belly whenever I stood up or stretched. My breasts swelled and I felt heavy and clumsy-footed as a calf. Initially it was only whispers behind clickety-flicking fans at the *mercado*, but then Papa locked the door and banned me from leaving the house.

One day, at about seven months, I crept out. The smell of blood was in the streets. A crowd was dispersing from the Plaza del Torres, leaving the corpse of the bull behind, while from across the street the statue of Carmen looked on, desolate. After pushing though the crowds for an hour, I turned homewards. I had nowhere else to go. My son came to me on a September day when the heat had matured into sultry warmth. The leaves along the Guadalquivir were starting to wither like old paper. I held my son only once before they took him away.

The next evening, careful not to be sighted, I stand at the corner of Plaza del Triumfo close to the Archivo del Indies and watch my son waiting in the spiked palm shade of the Alcazar Gardens. His expectant eyes scan the crowd and he holds his baseball cap in his hands. Something is eating the palms in Seville. Close to where I'm hiding, the palm trunk has been gnawed into a honeycomb of holes and is cordoned off in case the tree falls.

There are things my son will never know and things I cannot tell him. Like how I stood apart from the others on the night of Francesco's ordination, waiting in the silence under the jasmine tree. How the leaves were a dark mesh creeping over the church wall, and how the fading white blossoms parted their skirts to send the last of their heady sweetness into the still night air. I could never tell my son how, after I'd waited a long time, Francesco came to me. '*Ana*,' he said. His was voice rough as sea spray, as if something was caught it, or as if he was being choked by the clerical collar that now ringed his neck. Silently I plucked a wilting jasmine flower from a branch above my head and placed it in Francesco's palm. My son would never understand how Francesco's eyes still hold that same expression when he gives me the host each Sunday, although it's thirty-three years since we spoke alone. Or how after mass, I linger in the sacristy and carefully polish the chalice, listening to Francesco's voice as I dust my many gilded reflections.

I know my son will wait at the Alcazar Gardens all evening, and that he'll eventually retrace his steps to my apartment but I won't answer. I know he'll write to me and I'll reply saying that there's been a mistake, that he's not mine after all, and I know he'll be angry, but that he'll forgive me and return to his life. It's only now I realise the meaning of the dream sent by Virgin Maria del Carmen; that it did not herald my son's arrival, but his departure. My letting go. Returning to the blank page that awaits and the words elusive for so many years that will start to flow. Keeping to the shadows, I turn away and walk back up the hot street, into a heat haze that blurs and distorts the distance.

Roisín O'Donnell is an Irish writer whose work has been published in Ireland, the UK and Australia. Her family are from Derry and she grew up in Sheffield before moving to Ireland to study at Trinity College Dublin. On graduating with first class honours in English Studies, Roisín taught English abroad and travelled widely, spending time in South America and Spain, where 'Under the Jasmine Tree' was inspired.

She is presently teaching English at a university in Dublin, which she thoroughly enjoys as it gives her the opportunity to meet people from all over the world.

Roisín was recently shortlisted for the international Cúirt New Writing Prize 2014, the Wasafiri New Writing Prize 2014 -http://www.wasafiri.org/wasafiri-new-writing-prize.asp and has received an honorary mention in the Fish Flash Fiction Prize 2014. Her short stories and poems have appeared or are forthcoming in *Popshot Magazine*, *Colony Journal*, *Unthology* and *Structo* magazine.

Further stories are due to be anthologised in *Fugue: Contemporary Stories* (The Siren 2015), *Unfettered* (Tiny Owl, Brisbane) *and in Young Irelanders* (New Island, 2015). She lives in Dublin and is currently completing her first short story collection.

Lucy Luck commented:

'This is a well-constructed, well-told story with a beautiful sense of the heat of Seville, and an unsentimental but moving representation of love lost and a life of quiet resignation. The 1st person voice is nicely done.'

THE ACORN AWARD FOR AN UNPUBLISHED WRITER
MONA PORTE

The Crust

I grovel in the mud at his feet, the crust just out of reach. The pelting rain stings my skin and batters my eyes as I squint up at him.

Is this it? Is this my last moment on earth?

So, I straighten my stoop and give him as piercing a look as the rain will allow. I see in his eyes that he has seen the look in mine.

So, why doesn't he shoot?

A stoop and a squint. Reminds me of my father. The stoop from bending day after day to his precious work. The squint from years of wearing a monocle day in day out. It gave his once-kind face a village-idiot quality.

'Idiot!' I heard him shout, not for the first time, as a tray of tiny stones skittered across the floor, tinkling as they scattered. 'Now look what you've done! On my life, was ever a father so burdened with such a klutz. How will we find them all? Do you *know* how much these cost? What were you thinking?'

As if we didn't both know. Thoughts of my painting filled my head constantly. My brain saw dramatic, daring splashes of colour and communicated that to my arm movements.

'Hmm. Very good Ruben. You are not afraid to break with convention, I see. I like that,' said my art teacher. My teacher may have liked my brushstrokes of wild abandonment but my father would have preferred precision and delicacy. These were the qualities that would make me a good jeweller, like him. I just hadn't got the soul for gem-setting. I went through the motions like a badly calibrated machine, all the while longing to be set free.

'He's our only son,' pleaded my mother. 'Shouldn't we support what he wants to do in life?'

'But who will carry on the family business? I've spent my whole life building it up. I want to leave something behind. A legacy. That boy's head is in the clouds.'

'Yes, but this is *your* business, not his. Don't forget your father wanted you to carry on his tailoring business, but you went your own way,' she smiled. 'It was that streak of independence that attracted me to you. You were your own man. Couldn't we at least display some of his paintings in the shop, see if there's an appetite for them?'

And so it was. My paintings were displayed and caused quite a stir. People who liked beautiful jewellery also liked beautiful art. Men, even the *goyim*, came from far and wide to my father's shop to buy presents for their wives.

'Who is the artist?' asked Herr Eckhart, casting an appreciative eye around the walls.

'My son, Ruben.' My father made a lavish arm gesture in my direction. 'I am very proud of him.'

Ligner*!

'I came in for a necklace for my wife but perhaps I'll go home with a painting for myself. Or perhaps both.' He stopped in front of a painting of poor children playing in the streets. 'Called "Innocence" I see. I think you've captured that rather well. Wrap it for me please, mein Frau.' And so I sold my first painting.

'See!' hissed my mother from the back kitchen as the shop bell tinkled behind him. There was a lightness in her step as she laid the table with our lunch of cheese and unleavened bread.

The crust in the mud is not unleavened. I am past caring. I just want to reach it, feel its hardness mix with my saliva, and soften to slip down my throat like manna. The thought of this fills my head like a huge parachute, light and billowing, blotting out everything else. My brain has been possessed like this ever since I managed to liberate the crust early this morning. I watched a man die as he turned away from the line-up, collapsing like a burst balloon as though the extra effort involved in carrying the meagre ration was the final defeat. There was a scuffle as the lucky inmates nearby clambered over what had been our friend, scrabbling for the crust that had arced into the mud. My hand won by a sliver. I am slightly stronger than the others. Servers get the odd extra mouthful of slop.

Where to hide the crust?

I clutch it tight inside my bony palm for now, avoiding the envy-filled eyes as we are poked and prodded into line. Dead Zachary is dragged by the feet and flung in a pile for later burning. I long to eat my prize but eyes are everywhere. It is too precious to risk it being whipped away from me by the guards. I'd be shot for theft and the crust would be saved for the next meal.

Was there ever such an appetiser? The aroma of fresh-baked

challah fills my nostrils as, candles lit and *Kiddush* said, we sit down to Shabbat dinner.

'I sold two more paintings today, Mama.' I executed a victory wave with my fists. As my reputation spread by word of mouth, so did my pride.

'Be careful.' My father shook his head knowingly. 'You know the old Jewish proverb: "Pride is the mask we make of our faults".'

'Papa! Why must you spoil it for me? Do you begrudge me my talents?'

'No, but the Jews are a meek race. I'd just like to see you show some of that meekness.'

'Bow and scrape you mean? Be obsequious, like you? I can't stand it when I see you fawning before people. Like you are inferior.'

Where is my pride now? I try to dredge it up from somewhere deep inside me, but all I feel is the swooning frailty that hunger brings. The object of my desire is tantalizingly close, tormenting me with craving.

Which will be victorious in the end? Pride or hunger?

'Where have they gone?' I shouted, entering the shop and looking aghast at the pale rectangles on the wall, highlighting where the paintings once hung. Not one left.'

'They took them,' said Papa, his shoulders slumped.

'Who?'

'The Nazis, who else?'

'And you let them? You let them just walk in here and raid the place?'

'They came in here with their heel-clicking and their 'Heil Hitler' salutes. About five of them. What could I do? We are *old*, your Mama and me.'

'What trumped-up reason did they give anyway?'

'They called them "degenerate daubs". Said it was Party

policy to confiscate them, lest they sully the eyes and hearts of ordinary decent Germans.'

'Funny, he didn't think that when he bought them,' said Mama.

'Who? You're talking in riddles now,' I shouted.

'The Hauptmann. I recognised him. He was the one who bought your very first painting, and others afterwards. That was before they boycotted our businesses, of course. I remember him because of a scar on the back of his hand as he paid. Crescent-shaped, it was. A woman notices these things.'

'Couldn't you stop him, Papa? Couldn't you have done *something?*'

'Best to keep our heads down, keep out of trouble. That way they'll give up and leave us alone,' he said.

'Are you really that naïve, Papa? Even now, after all this time? There might have been some hope of that early on, but now they're like an unstoppable locomotive. There is nothing their propaganda *doesn't* blame us for: losing the war; causing the Great Depression. How illogical is that? They poison people's minds against us. We are an ugly, subversive breed. We want to take over the world just because we work hard in business. Oh, and let's not forget that we are natural carriers of diseases and so they must fight this *racial tuberculosis*. That Hitler is a maniac!'

'Sh-h! someone might hear you.' Papa darted furtive looks all around. 'We don't want to bring down any more wrath on our heads.'

'It's way too late for that! Haven't you heard they've built special camps for us?'

'Yes, but that's just for the homeless, the alcoholics, you know, the work-shy,' said Papa, waving his hand to dismiss the suggestion.

'And you really believe all that propaganda? Don't you find it just a little co-incidental how almost all these *work-shy* people just happen to be *Juden?*'

'How do you know that?'

'Er…Well, my friends tell me,' I said.

'What friends?'

'Well, friends of friends, really. They've infiltrated the camps, trying to rescue people.'

'Infiltrated? What friends are these?' He paused, realisation dawning. 'Don't tell me you're involved with the partisans?' he said, dropping his head into his hands as Mama started to weep.

'Not *actively* involved, no, but I sympathise with their aims…yes, and even their methods,' I shouted defensively. 'Desperate times require desperate measures.'

Like how I will manage to hide my crust. Hunger and weakness dull my brain, yet, like a ray of light in reverse, I hone in on the vital matter of the moment; the crust…that provider of life for another day. At the order, we queue up for the latrines. The splinters of the planks dig into my backside. Under cover of the flurry of trouser-dropping I slip the crust into my groin and try to trap it there between my testicles and inner thigh. Both are so emaciated I wonder if it'll hold.

If I shuffle as I walk, will it stay?

I try out my new gait and accidentally jostle the man in front of me. His spectacles fall off and I hear the scrunch under my feet.

Glass everywhere. *Kristallnacht.* Our shop window reduced to smithereens, tiny as the gems inside, spewing across pavements like so many shattered dreams. Stormtroopers attacking Jewish shops and synagogues, wielding sledgehammers with unleashed venom, spurred on by the screams which rent the air. Carnage. Flames licking high into the sky as they plundered and desecrated. They died that night, Mama and Papa, along with eighty-nine others. Bludgeoned to death with hammers. I found their mangled bodies the next day, lying on a bed of glass in the ransacked shop. That was my last image of them, etched into my brain;

wild gaping bloody chasms in their heads, Mama's skirts up round her waist.

Did Papa put up some token resistance in the end? Did he die because of my insults, my exhortations? And where was I?
Off with the partisans, putting up noble resistance. Much good did it do me. I still ended up in the camp.

The guard steps forward and shoots the myopic man in the head. My stumble signed his death warrant. A short-sighted worker is no use to them. Not worth feeding any longer. We are being herded together to be addressed by the new Obergruppenfuhrer. His reputation has spread shivers of fear rippling round the camp. I have to side-step the carcass.

Will this wider step dislodge my hidden feast? I concentrate hard on a tiny crab-wise movement. *Will it fool them?* My pulse quickens. I can feel the rasping of the rough crust in my groin, at once a comfort and a torment. I can see my breath in the cold morning air, yet sweat erupts on my brow. *Will they notice it?* I hold my breath. My vision swirls.

'Hey…you, Jew,' a guard shouts, pointing at me. His eyes narrow.

I am discovered. I force my breathing to normality. The crust grates like sandpaper.

Ignore it! And the pounding in your head. It will surely burst in a second and my brains will gush forth onto the guard's feet.
I stand a yard away from him, my eyes lowered. A sliver of my vision sees his arm stretch out. *Holding a gun?* He reaches out and strikes his match on my stubbly head, guffawing as I flinch and almost topple over, partly from his pressure and partly from relief.

I am giddy with relief. As I slither on my way I can scarce concentrate on my task of concealment. I start to shake uncontrollably and my taut muscles loosen. All of them. As I stand right in front of the Obergruppenfuhrer, the crust betrays me and slips down my leg. I feel its treacherous path.

Like a silver trail left by a snail. I try to clench up to stop it but it is past the point of return. It plops gently onto the slimy ground as the whole line is pushed back a few paces and lies there, staring accusingly up at me. I think to put out my foot to cover it but my brain will not communicate with my limbs. I sink to my knees.

'Dieb**!' barks the Obergruppenfuhrer, stepping forward, his jackboots right in front of me, laden with doom. I squint up at him as he seems to hesitate, puzzled. He pulls off his gauntlet, reaching towards his holster and I notice a crescent-shaped scar on his hand. Like a bullet to the brain, understanding hits me. I straighten my stoop and shout,

'I am Ruben Freedman, Herr Eckhart, painter of degenerate daubs!'

He aims. An explosion of taste fills my brain, delighting all my senses; challah, chicken soup, gefilte fish, lockshen pudding... The Promised Land.

*Ligner** Liar
*Dieb*** Thief

Mona Porte began her working life as a teacher of languages but later became a specialist teacher of children with dyslexia. This she embraced with a passion, although it led to the deterioration of her own spelling! Her mother always maintained that Mona 'had a book in her' so, when she gave up teaching a few years ago, this remembered comment prompted her to return to creative writing, an activity which she had enjoyed at school and college.

She has written many short stories but has never offered any of them for publication. She has been longlisted/shortlisted a number of times in competitions but has never won a prize until now, apart from in a very small local competition. She is currently working on a novel so perhaps it is time for that 'book' her mother saw to emerge. She lives on the Dorset coast but frequently visits her native Ireland. She enjoys walking on cliff-tops and dancing, both jive and tap.

The BSSA longlist judges commented:

'The intensity of the story lives on in our minds. We were impressed at how it works on several levels which increases its poignancy and makes it more powerful than other stories on this theme.'

EMILY BULLOCK

Zoom

It starts in darkness. Then the interior light comes on.

A boy sits in the front passenger seat. He twists round to say something to a younger boy in the back. It zooms in closer. The car is gone, just two faces at the window. The younger boy is wearing Spiderman pyjamas. The zoom wobbles; it makes the boys look like they are shaking. The older boy faces forward again. Why doesn't he see it coming?

You have been filming them for two weeks. The school assignment was called Getting to Know Your Neighbours. You were supposed to interview them but the farm on the left was empty; even the For Sale sign was broken. And the neighbours on the right: Mrs Phipps and the boys had moved out last summer; Mr Phipps was always working in the fields that surrounded the house. So, you took to filming them instead like one of those Attenborough programmes your dad watched on boxed sets.

This is the third time of watching. The zoom is good enough to show the younger boy playing with the straps of his car seat. He looks nearly big enough to use a grown-up belt, but he won't ever get that chance. The clip plays on a loop.

Nothing much happened until last weekend. Mrs Phipps had dropped the boys at the gate; she never went up to the house anymore. The boys got half-way down before they saw it. The black bull was out, wedged under the hedge like a huge meteor fallen to earth. Mr Phipps shouting from the house. Mrs Phipps screaming from her car. The bull lifted its heavy head; big as a black hole in the hawthorn. You filmed it all from your bedroom window.

Mrs Phipps won. The boys ran back to her; they drove off and didn't stay for their weekend visit. The car was a safe place that day.

Here comes the next bit already.

The mike isn't good enough to pick up sound but the man outside the car must be speaking. The older boy, the one in front, reaches down to undo his belt. He leans to the right, flicking the car headlights on. The zoom lurches up. The fenland slips into grey, a purple glow surrounding Boston Stump like a bruise. It drops back to the car. The younger boy yawns, scratching at the neck of his Spiderman pyjamas. Why aren't they in bed?

That morning Mr Phipps had a delivery of sheep. Something to record at last. You took Sammy to see them in the field opposite. Keep that dog away from my stock, Mr Phipps said. But Sammy was always on a lead, not like the Alsatian from the weekend cottages down the road. Twelve years old, tall for your age, but his snout reached your stomach. That dog chased you whenever you rode your bike past, snapping and snarling, and always barked when Mr Phipps fired cartridge-scarers up into the sky.

You went back to the gate, filming from behind a telephone pole; zooming in. Mr Phipps talking to your dad about the sheep like they were his babies, all soft and cooing: how the price of lamb was on the up, how he was going to make a killing. Do up the farm and get them all back on their feet, get back his wife and his boys.

Mr Phipps said things were going to happen. Mr Phipps said he was sure of it.

It stays with the two boys, in profile, like a shot from 'You've Been Framed': waiting for a monkey to steal a

windscreen wiper, for someone to jump out wearing a
monster mask. But none of those things are going to happen.
No laughter track, no music, no voiceover, no caption
– footage contains some images that viewers may find
disturbing. It is going to happen. It will happen soon.

It zooms out. The man is moving around the car; bending
down then bobbing up again further away in the field. The
younger boy's head drops forward. He is asleep. The older
boy in front leans his chin on the dashboard, tracing his finger
across the windscreen. He must be cold, or he is playing
make-believe, because he lifts the hood of his Nike sweater
over his head. His face becomes a black hole.

*It was the night of the predicted meteor shower. You had set
your alarm for 11.30pm, in case you fell asleep; practising the shot
through the bedroom window. A new man had dropped Mr Phipps'
boys off for their weekend visit. But nothing else happened and you
waited for it to get dark. The wind came off the Wash, sweeping the
clouds away towards the Midlands. A clear view straight up into
the sky. No trees or hills to break the flat farmland that stretched and
stretched.*

Still the interior light and the two boys: one sleeping, one
running his fingers, like short pumping legs, along the dash.
The older boy checks the car clock; the time can't be seen from
this angle. The zoom moves again. He sets to drumming,
glancing over his shoulder. The younger boy sleeps on, hands
jerking; he must be dreaming. Neither boy gets up to see what
is happening outside the car. Would things be different if they
did?

*You had zoomed in and out, getting the focus right. Your
dad hadn't even noticed his Smartphone was missing. Your sister
already asleep in the bed furthest from the door, the nightlight
shining on her face. You turned away from the window and zoomed
in on your sister: mouth gulping, eyelashes fluttering. You took it
even closer into a blur of pink and red flesh. The zoom was strong
enough to record the whole thing.*

The man's face appears again, this time at the back of the

car. The older boy looks up. The boot opens and shuts. The face is gone. Things look different at night. But the boy must know the man because he slides over to the driver's seat and waves. He opens the door, facing away from the camera now. His padded coat, bulked out with the sweater underneath, looks like a harlequin print but that is only the light. He sits back; the coat becomes navy blue again.

You noticed that everything looked different at night, dipped in blue: the hawthorn bush next door like a giant bony hand, fingers spread open in defence; the RAF landing lights at the end of the field like red Chinese lanterns blown off course. The sheep were stone still, illuminated by moonlight; no streetlamps that far out of the village. You had thought then that the sheep must be deep sleepers like your sister, but it turned out that you were wrong.

It shows the older boy putting one hand on the wheel as if he is driving it. He steers carefully and he would have made a good driver. His hand imagines the move of changing gears, or at least his shoulder, visible through the window, echoes this movement. The hood slips down a little. Dark close cut hair grows low on his forehead or perhaps he is frowning.

Soon the meteor would pass close enough to shatter into a thousand or more shooting stars over earth. You started recording.

Lights moved over Mr Phipps' field, the one in front of the house. The Alsatian was barking; running away from the sheep field, along the top of the dyke. Maybe it had started early. But it was only a car turning off the road and onto the track. Headlights bumping along, but it was too dark to see who was inside. The car stopped.

Then the interior light came on.

The older boy slips his hands inside his pockets. It is getting cold. He yawns and checks the clock again. He is the sensible one; he knows it is past their bedtime. The zoom catches the man outside the car. It looks like he is carrying a stick; lifting it up to point at something in the dark.

The zoom follows the man back to the car. The older boy sits up straight.

That small movement is familiar: the nod as the boy

returns to the passenger seat for the final time. How many times has it been now?

It was still playing; loop after loop. The zoom had been strong enough to record the whole thing. But this time you didn't want to see it alone. Clouds blacked out the moon; there would be no meteor shower tonight. You moved away from the window; needed to share it, to have someone else watch it too. To make sure it was realer than one of those nightmares where your legs turned to stone and your mouth filled with cotton wool; or one of those horror films where the action slowed and the camera entered with the bullet.

It will happen soon: the older boy in front, the younger boy asleep in the red and black car seat; the man pushing his head so it is just inside the door.

The light shows Mr Phipps and his boys.

You ran across the room, landing with a thud on the Peppa Pig duvet set. Your sister turned over, grunting, burying her face in the pillow. You grabbed her shoulders, shook her awake. Pulled her up into a sitting position; shaking again until her eyes rolled open.

This is it.

The man holds up the thick black stick but it isn't a stick. The shotgun flashes. The boy slumps back against the passenger door, glass shatters into a thousand cubes of light. The zoom shakes as if it feels the ricochet. The hood slips back from what is left of the boy's face. Blood stains the windscreen black.

The younger brother wakes. He scratches at the seat straps trapping him, just as he did in sleep. But now his eyes are open. The shot kills him before he opens his mouth. His arms and legs fly up and fall back as if the car has been hit from behind by an articulated-lorry. The straps keep his body in place. He doesn't slide out of view like his older brother has.

The interior light goes off; but it doesn't end yet. There is a third flash. The zoom doesn't shake this last time. It settles on the dead sheep scattered in the field, throats torn out.

That's not real, your sister said. Did you get it off the net, she said. Is it top ranked on YouTube, she said. You tell your sister you found it. Where, she said. You pointed to the window. All the sound in the world came back

Now. So loud even Mrs Phipps, ten miles away in Boston, must be able to hear. Your sister screams and screams; screams and screams.

Emily Bullock won the Bristol Short Story Prize with her story 'My Girl', which was also broadcast on BBC Radio 4. She worked in film before pursuing writing full time. Her memoir piece 'No One Plays Boxing' was shortlisted for the Fish International Publishing Prize 2013. She also won the National Writers in Education Conference (NAWE) Short Story Competition in 2013. She has a Creative Writing MA from the University of East Anglia and completed her PhD at the Open University, where she also teaches Creative Writing.

Her debut novel *The Longest Fight* will be published by Myriad in Spring 2015. www.emilybullock.com / @ emilybwriting

SHORTLISTED
HELEN COOPER

Pretending to Know the Words

Luis had not moved in a while. He was slumped on a wide leather sofa, gazing at his reflection in a blank plasma screen. He imagined phoning his mother, all those miles away, and saying something strange. Something like, this giant house hates me.

She would say, don't talk crazy. Has that English air sent you mad?

He would say, my feet are cold on the glossy floorboards. The bed makes me feel as if I'm drowning. I am a speck in this shiny house. And it hates me for being ungrateful.

He jolted as he realised he was about to hit the floor. The slippery sofa was rejecting him, sliding him off. He hauled himself back, but now that his trance was broken, the silence pressed. He jabbed at the remote control to wake the television, and winced at the fierce colours of Match of the Day.

Vague ideas of changing the channel lolled around his

brain. But when a scarlet number 17 shirt flooded the picture, his eyes locked on. Recoba was written beneath the number. Luis' lips twitched with the name, while, onscreen, the striker weaved across a vivid green pitch. The ball seemed to hover at his feet, until it rocketed through the air to balloon the back of the net.

Recoba's celebration was shown close up, in slow motion. His mouth inched into a roar, his lips shrank back, his dark eyes glittered. He seemed to be experiencing something so pure and primitive that Luis felt a burn of envy. His vision began to fuzz. The commentator's voice hummed through the sound system. 'One day of fixtures left... four points separate the top three teams…next weekend is going to be one of the most exciting ends to a season we've seen...'

In the studio, the pundits argued about who would win the League. Every time they mentioned Recoba, the leather grew colder against Luis' spine. He thought again of his mother. Imagined pressing the phone to his ear, listening to her voice, her language. But she would be angry with him for not calling in so long. He couldn't cope with it tonight.

Instead he dragged himself off the sofa and into his kitchen. The room winked black and chrome. He floundered for a moment, then strode to the corner and wrenched a knife from a silver holder. He rested the point on the back of his hand; let it tremble there before he made a small gasp of a cut. The sharp pain was just what he'd wanted. He watched scarlet blood leak onto the worktop.

It was time. Recoba flexed his fists as he waited in the tunnel, feeling the clench and release of the muscles in his arms. From above came the thumping anticipation of the crowd. In front were the restless outlines of his teammates, rolling their shoulders and shifting from foot to foot. Recoba should have felt connected to them in these charged final moments. He had clashed skulls with them as they'd leapt for headers; pressed shoulders in free kick walls; seen them pale and naked in the shower. But still they felt like aliens.

He looked away from them, stripping his mind of everything but the game. If they won, and their nearest rivals didn't, they would be champions. Champions of the English Premier League. It was what he had dreamed of when he was young, playing on a breezy pitch in Uruguay with his brother and their friends.

The signal came. As he and his teammates streamed onto the pitch, Recoba braced himself. Sometimes he worried he wouldn't be able to cope with the surge of energy and desire that swept him during a match. He feared the crash would come too early. But when the starting whistle shrieked, there was only his body, and the ball, and the dancing formations of the other players. Recoba leapt for overhead shots, feet scissoring the sky, the ball pounding against the crossbar. He took curving, near-perfect free kicks, grinding his jaw as the goalkeeper's fingertips denied him.

When his real chance came, he felt it. He knew that Wade wanted to pass to him; knew that a small but perfect space was opening up ahead. He slipped into the gap, turning to meet the ball, foot connecting, ball soaring, slamming into the net. The crowd rose to its feet in a scarlet blur. Recoba stormed the length of the pitch, roaring and pounding his chest, while his team mates fell into an ecstatic tangle somewhere behind.

As play re-started, he glanced at the clock. Seven minutes to go. Coach was yelling from the sidelines that their challengers for the League were only drawing. Recoba tossed his head and wiped sweat from his eyes. He'd once overheard a team mate say, Recoba gets a right scary look towards the end of a game. Recoba didn't care. They just had to hold on, hold on.

When the final whistle trilled, it took him a few moments to stop moving; to collect in the parts of himself that seemed to have scattered across the pitch. He became conscious of a rising chant from the crowd. RecoBA RecoBA RecoBA. An image of Luis burst into his mind. Sitting on a leather sofa, looking as blank as the walls of his house. Recoba shook it away and steamed down the pitch, arms flung wide, fleeing the other players as they tailed him like excited muggers.

The dressing room fizzed. Players flicked towels at one another and hollered songs Recoba had never heard. He sat on a bench and looked at his shaking hands, balling his fists to contain the adrenaline that seemed to be oozing from him.

'Hey Reco, you coming into town?'

Recoba lifted his head. Summerfield, the freckled centre-back, was standing with a towel around his waist, grinning at him. Recoba struggled to translate the smile. Sometimes he suspected that even facial expressions meant something different here.

'I...I'm not sure...'

'Come on, Reco. We've won the league! You're the hero!'

Recoba shook his head. 'Not me.'

'So fuckin' modest! Get dressed! We're champiooooons!'

Recoba slackened with exhaustion. His body was beginning to feel like a sack of sand he would have to drag around. But maybe he could go with them. For once, perhaps he should go.

'Well...maybe one drink.'

They marched out of the backdoor as a singing, clapping army. Recoba trailed behind. Panic jumped into his throat when he saw the queue of black limousines. He found himself jostled into one, trapped in a leather-lined space with squad members he'd never spoken to. They rocked the car and doused its seats with champagne. Recoba moved his lips to give the impression he knew their tuneless songs.

When the car pulled up, he scrambled out, gulping in air as if hauling himself out of a river. But he slipped into a rushing current of designer suits; was swept down a cobbled street. He didn't recognise this part of the city. He allowed himself to be guided to a black door studded with white lights. A bouncer swung it open, nodding at the players as they streamed in. 'Blindin' goal today, Mr. Recoba.'

RecoBA RecoBA RecoBA. He tried to recall how the stadium had vibrated with that name not so long ago. But Luis' warning voice filled his head, hissing that he had no business in a place like this. Recoba stalled in the doorway. Somebody nudged him in the back, and he spilled into the room.

The bar was low-lit and noisy. A fountain spat champagne. Women were perched on stools, wearing backless dresses, skin like hard, gleaming caramel. In one corner, people lurched to the music. The air was tinged with sweat, but it smelt alcoholic and vaguely perfumed.

Recoba's teammates were led into a shadowy, roped-off area. He hung back, watching them slide into red booths, watching a waitress with a sweep of black hair pour champagne. He knew he would leave. His teammates had made it too easy; they were tipping fizz into each other's mouths and wouldn't notice him creep away.

The footage of the league winners' celebrations was being shown again. Luis watched Recoba leaping up and down, sandwiched between two teammates, the silver cup shining above. His expression was different to the one he'd worn in earlier scenes, when they'd shown him tearing along the pitch by himself. Luis couldn't stir his brain enough to analyse the distinction. Nor could he feel even a spark of excitement. Recoba had earned him this house, this furniture, the car in the drive. Yet Luis couldn't summon anything close to gratitude.

He ran his eyes over the row of painkillers on the coffee table. He had been collecting them over the past week, buying two packets a day. Their presence in his cupboard had felt comforting. A possibility.

Tonight he had got them out and lined them up.

Recoba watched the ball sail towards him, arcing through the air. It glowed as if it was on fire. He bent his knees, pushed from his calves, felt his feet leave Earth. His head connected with the ball, but he didn't tumble back down. He kept soaring until the sky was bleached of colour.

Luis jolted with the sensation of falling. Fragments of a dream cascaded away, and his eyes flickered, catching glimpses of a white room.

'Reco,' said a voice.

Luis swam up through hazy layers. His head swirled. There was a clawing pain in his stomach, and a fluorescent light trying to burn his retinas. 'I...'

'Take it easy, man. Just rest.'

Luis turned his head, pain shooting through. He could tell now that he was in hospital. Next to his bed, in a black suit and crumpled pink shirt, was Summerfield.

He tried to focus. 'What...'

'You took some pills.'

Snatches of memory floated back. A door twinkling with cold stars. Champagne frothing aggressively. A calming wall of aspirin boxes. Tears stung in Luis' eyes.

Summerfield leaned forward. 'After you left the bar without saying anything, the others just reckoned you were being your usual mysterious self. But I had this feeling... I recognised the signs...'

'Signs?'

'It's more common than you think.'

'I... what is?'

'I know what you've been telling yourself. How can you be depressed, when you're a rich footballer in the Prem? Well...' Summerfield shrugged and seemed awkward for a moment, 'you can. And you probably feel guilty for not being deliriously fuckin' happy. But it happens. Only nobody talks about it...'

Luis blinked, struggling to absorb Summerfield's words. Everything felt slow, dream-like.

'Is there somebody I can call for you?' Summerfield asked, 'Family in Uruguay?'

Summerfield knew his country. Luis had always imagined the other players calling him 'the South American.' He swiped at his eyes. 'No. Thank you. I'll call them.'

Summerfield stood up. 'I'll to leave you to rest, then. Doc should be coming soon. But when you get out of here, we'll talk. You've got to talk about it. Otherwise it just gets...you know...'

As the door closed behind his teammate, Luis stared up at the white ceiling. His thoughts slipped and slid, moments of clarity blaring out of the fog. He saw Recoba pounding a ball into a net, making a stadium riot into life. He saw Luis, off the pitch, senses deadened, with no idea who he was supposed to be.

As the images bled into one another, his eyes drooped closed. Now he brought his mother's face to mind, blurred at first, but sharpening, brightening, filling him with longing. He would phone her when he woke. And he would say, I don't know how to be a real person in this country.

And she would say, don't talk crazy.

And he would say, remind me who I am.

And she would say, in her telling-off voice, Luis Recoba, I haven't got time for riddles.

Helen Cooper lives in Derby with her husband and works at the University of Birmingham as an Academic Writing Advisor. Her commute gives her a daily window of lovely writing time.

One of her earliest memories is of writing a surreal story about turning into a tortoise, and it being performed in assembly. For years after that, she embarked on a different novel every week, resulting in notebooks full of first chapters. It was only when she did an MA in Creative Writing at Nottingham Trent University that she learnt how to finish things.

Since then she has completed one novel and almost finished a second. She was longlisted in the *Mslexia* Novel Competition in 2011 and shortlisted for the Yeovil Literary Prize in 2013. Her stories have appeared in *Writers' Forum* and the *Lincolnshire Echo*. She couldn't be without her brilliant writers' group, who keep her prose on its toes.

Lucy Luck commented:

'It is very difficult to write well about football, and this story manages it elegantly and effectively. Good characterisation and an interesting take on the loneliness of fame.'

K M ELKES

Greta Garbo and the Chrysanthemum Man

That Greta Garbo woman, her from number 18, is a stinking old witch who hasn't left her flat for five years. Lily Woo, from two doors down and newly moved in, learns all this from the other neighbours. She learns some new words too: 'crackpot' and 'right weirdo'. Lily Woo thinks it is always good to learn new things.

At first, when she steps outside her flat and walks along the damp, echoing concrete landing, Lily hurries past Greta Garbo Woman's grubby door and the faint smell of cigarette smoke, fearing the old woman will scuttle out.

Lily imagines clotted grey hair and bare feet, uncut toenails tick-tick-ticking on the ground. Spidery hands and one clouded eye with a pin-point pupil. She remembers her grandfather's story of the witch of Ye on the River Zhang. How she would chose maidens from the villages to become a bride for the river god. They were dressed in the finest silks, her grandfather said, then bound tightly to beautifully decorated rafts that would sink into the dark water before the young girls could even scream.

Lily doesn't want to be caught by a witch. She definitely doesn't want to be a bride again.

What Lily wants is to be left alone, separated from what had gone before, like a boat quietly leaving a dock. There is a job cleaning hotel rooms, occasional emails from her cousin in Hong Kong, the view over the rooftops in the late, grey mornings when she returns from work. These, she thinks, are the compromises of failure.

Two weeks after she moves in, Lily walks along the landing (she has forgotten to hurry now) when That Greta Garbo Woman speaks from the dark space behind her door: 'My dear, are you the new lady from number 16?'

Lily is wise. She knows how to hear something and not turn around, not to be taken in by a simple question that may lead to others. She knows how to move on without a pause, soft-footed, like a spirit. She doesn't stop and only shudders one floor down.

She hears the old woman ask the same question for three days in a row, without ever pausing, until there is silence again.

Lily is glad, she doesn't want to get involved. Getting involved she has already done. She thinks about the man she had to marry, how angry he was. Not always with her, but something, how he looked for anger, searching around the house they shared, the bed.

And there was always that question, stabbed into her each month: 'Why no son? Why?'

One evening, while she is trying to learn new things from the television (but still does not understand why the dramas they show so often are set in estates just like the one she lives in), Lily sees a man walk by along the landing. He pauses by her window to adjust his jacket, run a finger through thinning hair. She has not seen this stranger before, would have remembered him if she had. He is big bellied, teeth like tombstones, carrying a small, scraggy bunch of chrysanthemums in one hand, a folded stool in the other.

His shirt is buttoned to the top, but no tie, a double crease in each of his trousers. There is a noticeable swagger in his step, a joyous arch of the foot as he walks on.

He stops two doors up and rings the bell. Lily opens the door, peeks out. From out of That Greta Garbo Woman's doorway comes a hand. The man takes it in his and with tenderness bends and kisses the fingers. With a flourish he unfolds his stool, sits, and passes the tired flowers through, one by one.

Lily retreats inside her flat, wondering at such at a tender moment, surprised the old woman could ever have found such a devoted man. She listens by the door, hears conversation bubbling like water in a pan, then hears laughter, a woman's, bright and clear as mountain water. She thinks how strange such noise sounds in the solemn quiet of her flat.

The next time Lily passes two doors up, reaches the stairwell, pauses, then turns back. She rings the bell and hears a rustle and shuffle. The door opens a few inches. Lily can see a sliver of hallway, nicotine stains on the wall, there is a musty smell, but not unpleasant, like the old shop where her grandfather would go to buy plum-flavoured tobacco for his pipe.

Lily thinks that Old Greta Garbo Woman must spend a lot of time looking out through the fish eye. There is a face barely visible in the gloom, bright-eyed, smiling.

'You want something from shop?' Lily asks the darkened entrance and the kite tails of smoke that curl from it.

'Please, I'd be so grateful,' the voice is cracked, but gentle.

Around the door comes a crumpled piece of paper — a shopping list — and then a ten pound note. The hand is pale and bony. Lily giggles at the thought of witches, that old story of sacrifice. And then she remembers the chrysanthemum man, such happiness on his face, the tenderness with which he kissed those delicate fingers.

When she returns Lily rings the bell then leaves the shopping by the door. She walks to her own flat, and pauses, waiting to see what emerges, two doors down. Nothing moves for a while. There is just the sound of the wind along the landing, the high, raised voices of children in the playground across the road. Still Lily stands, more curious than wary.

The door opens, a long, black-sleeved arm, elegant and frail comes out, picks up the bag and pulls it inside.

'Thank you,' says That Old Greta Garbo Woman, then: 'My name is Rebecca.'

'I am Lily.'

'Welcome Lily,' says Rebecca, 'Welcome.'

Lily goes back into her flat, puts on the kettle to make green tea, and whispers the new word she has learned, over and again: 'Welcome'.

And as she looks out over the rooftops, Lily realises, for the first time, how beautiful they look, shining in the rain.

K M Elkes is a prize-winning author, print journalist and backpacking traveller from Bristol, UK. Since starting to write fiction seriously in 2011 he has won the 2013 Fish Publishing Flash Fiction Prize and been shortlisted twice for the Bridport Prize.

His work has also appeared in various anthologies and won prizes at *Words With Jam*, *Momaya Review*, *Writing WM*, *Lightship Publishing* and *Accenti* in Canada. His flash fiction stories have appeared on websites including Everyday Fiction, Waterhouse Review, Litro and East of the Web.

Ken tweets via @mysmalltales and blogs at www. kmelkes.co.uk.

BARBARA FEATHERSTONE

The Radiant Girl

Sister Mary shifted uncomfortably in her confining habit. It had been a long, hot, and tedious afternoon. A bead of sweat trickled down her back, an unwelcome dampness prickling her armpits. Her aching feet in her black-laced shoes felt like flat, smelly kippers as she helped shepherd Father O'Brien's chattering flock about the 'New Gymnasium'.

Half an hour later, the flock spilled from the fusty interior of the gym onto the sunlit lawns of St. Bridget's Convent School. Sister Mary rounded up the strays, and edged back into the shadows of the doorway. She harrumphed thankfully. Only one more exhibit to endure.

'As you are all aware…' Father O'Brien cleared his throat. The chatter faded to an expectant silence, '…it was our respected benefactor, the late Lady Gilroy, whose so very generous bequest has enabled us to create such splendid improvements to St. Bridget's.'

There was a confusion of bowed heads and a smattering of applause for the departed. The Sister's glance roamed the gaggle of senior girls, parents, teaching Sisters and dignitaries. The men were cool in lightweight suits and open-necked shirts, prepared for the seasonal weather. Jackets were carried over an arm, or hooked casually with one finger over a shoulder. Girls and women wore sleeveless dresses, sandals, flowery sunhats and dark glasses.

Sister Mary sighed, a sudden yearning to feel cool grass once more between bare toes, lemon sunlight on her face, creamy wavelets dancing about her naked limbs. She shook the yearnings from her. She had made her bed. A long time ago.

Father O'Brien mopped his brow with a large, creased white handkerchief. 'And now, dear friends, our tour is drawing sadly to a close. I think you will all agree that this has been an instructive and pleasurable afternoon. If you could bear with me just a little longer...'

Sister Mary listened idly. A movement from the fringe of the gathering caught her attention. She watched Cindy Flannery, one of the senior girls, sidle off across the lawn towards the rose garden. The girl's tangle of dark tresses hung loose, shoes dangling from her hand, dress hitched up; the hem barely skimming the top of her ample thighs. And *her* a representative of St Bridget's.

She'd be having a strong word in that young lady's ear. And that Ryan Kelly, the gardener's boy, no better. Secateurs dropping uselessly into his wheelbarrow, as Cindy reached the rose garden and darted towards him. Almost drooling, the lad was. Forgotten all about dead-heading the roses. That was two strong words she'd be having.

She searched discreetly for someone to help. Sister Theresa was closest. She moved a step forward and tried to catch her eye. But Sister Theresa was oblivious to her appeal, gazing up enraptured at Father O'Brien as his gaze wandered affectionately over his flock.

Sister Mary folded her arms, hands tucked into the long sleeves of her robe; noting the Father's gaze rest just a tad more lingeringly on the rosy cheeks of Sister Theresa. She harrumphed again. Blushing cheeks meant impure thoughts. And as for Father O'Brien... There'd be no sense in seeking help from that quarter. Like a lovelorn lamb, the Father was. Not that Sister Theresa needed any encouragement. Even as a girl she'd been the flighty one.

The Sister's mind spun back thirty years, back to Galway. They'd lived two doors apart. Laouise O'Mara and Clodagh Murphy they were then, before they were 'reborn'. Two little girls, as close as sisters, running wild the day. Twirling their rat tail skipping ropes, knocking at doors for a cup of milk; sand in their shoes, and dirt on their faces.

Sister Mary sniffed. Laouise... 'radiant girl', the name meant. And she was the radiant girl. Eyes the blue of the bay. And that glorious mane of hair – gold as treacle, it was, and rippling right down to her bottom. All the boys lusting after her. And Patrick, her big brother, looking on, as proud as proud. 'Itchy feet,' they called Patrick O'Mara. Always on the move that one, as restless as a flea.

When Patrick O'Mara's itchy feet danced him away from Galway to fresher fields, no one was surprised. Though they were surprised when, not long after, Clodagh Murphy departed, too. Alone, she found herself wandering from place to place; always searching, never knowing what it was she was seeking. Eventually, she entered the religious life and discovered some kind of contentment. Until, that was, she was transferred to St. Bridget's Convent School and found Laouise O'Mara installed before her; Sister Theresa as she was now.

She'd not kept up the childhood ties. In small moments, she imagined the 'radiant girl' blissfully wed, with a brood of golden children. Maybe Patrick, too, though with his itchy feet still dancing. Now the anguish and the restlessness had started up all over again. That mane of gold hair, shorn and hidden now beneath a snowy headdress. Those eyes, Patrick's eyes, the blue of the bay. Laouise and Patrick O'Mara, they'd been two peas in a pod.

Sister Mary sleeved a glisten of sweat from her brow. She must learn to be more humble, more charitable, and to 'count her blessings'. It was too late for anything else. She nudged herself from the shadowy doorway and followed the yawning flock as they were ushered swiftly on, across lush lawns, down gravelled paths, and around the tennis court.

Father O'Brien was mopping his brow again, the handkerchief now looking considerably damp and bedraggled. 'I thank you all, dear people, for your patience. Though I am sure everyone has appreciated this delightful opportunity to view such numerous and interesting improvements to St Bridget's.'

Sister Mary huffed. Cindy Flannery wasn't appreciating the opportunity. All that young miss was appreciating was skiving off to canoodle with the gardener's boy.

The priest returned the limp handkerchief to his pocket. With a majestic sweep of the arm, Father O'Brien encompassed his flock. 'We come now to our magnificent finale. Refreshments will be served afterwards on the terrace.'

There was a faint murmur of relief.

'Ladies and gentlemen, Sisters, girls – I give you – the Japanese Water Garden! Inspiration of our dear…of…er… Sister Theresa.' He coughed, casting the Sister a beatific smile.

Sister Theresa fluttered her eyelashes in demure delight, flushed a delicate pink, and cast her gaze modestly to the ground. The tour began, the priest's words rising and falling like softly coloured butterflies amongst the flowers. The tinkling sound of the water fountain soothed the senses. Jasmine and mimosa scented the air as the gathering swarmed over the quaint little bridge, across the koi pond, to the oriental charms of the pagoda.

Sister Mary started after them. At the koi pond she paused. She looked over the rail of the little bridge into the water. *Was it the heat, or the tiredness?* She was dizzy, her thoughts fizzing like sparkling lemonade. She wanted to slip into that cooling water, shroud herself in its sensuous silkiness, and then dry herself with sunshine…

'Are you all right, Sister? You're not looking at all yourself.'

Herself? What was herself?

It was Sister Theresa – Laouise O'Mara that was.

'I'm fine, Sister, that I am. I was watching the fish, that's all.'

The two Sisters joined the entourage dotted about the pagoda. Father O'Brien was still spouting; gesticulating; exonerating the virtues, the creativity, and the inspirational imagination of Sister Theresa. There were polite nods, tight smiles, glazed eyes, and a gradual drifting away…

Father O'Brien blinked, gazing about him, as if awakening from a reverie. 'Everyone is leaving.' He recovered quickly. 'Sure, and hasn't it been a great success? A grand day.' Another beatific smile, a flick of the cassock, and he, too, was gone.

Side by side, the two Sisters made their way out of the garden, separated by just the most miniscule of spaces. As they reached the new gymnasium Sister Mary paused. The gym was her special responsibility. She took a key from her pocket. 'I'll be checking inside before I lock up.' She motioned towards the Convent. 'I'll catch you up, Sister. One pair of eyes is all that's needing.'

Sister Theresa took only a few steps, and swivelled back. 'Sure, this sun's rather strong. It'll be cooler inside, I'm thinking. And two pairs of eyes are better than one.'

There was a sniff followed by a grunt.

Sister Mary turned, squinting from the sunlight into the dimness of the gymnasium. A shadow moved.

'It's that eejit Ryan Kelly. He must have slipped in unnoticed. You can't be trusting the boy. Let's hope he hasn't got that Cindy Flannery in there with him. I saw the pair of them canoodling earlier. I tried to warn you, Sister Theresa, so I did. But you were too busy fluttering your lashes at the Father.'

She moved forward into the gym. 'You shouldn't be in here, Ryan Kelly!'

The creak of the exercise bike and desperate panting answered her. The gardener's boy was alone. She regarded the glistening jowls, the sweat darkened hair, the blue-jeaned buttocks squelching over the saddle.

'Got to get me fat down, Sister. Me Dad says I'm not fit to heave a wheelbarrow.' He flicked the two nuns a mischievous grin. 'Besides, a girl prefers a fellow with a bit of muscle. That's what Cindy Flannery said. And I've a mind to catch that Cindy.'

The Sisters shooed him out.

They moved down to the row of exercise bikes, their robes softly swishing. Sister Theresa mopped her forehead. 'Sure, and it's hot. Take the weight off your feet, Sister.' She whisked up her skirts, mounted a bike, and began to pedal.

Sister Mary scowled. 'And aren't you the common one? And flirting like that with the Father! You made a holy show of yourself, so you did.' She hitched up her own skirts and clambered astride the adjoining machine, shoving down hard on the pedals. 'Even as a girl you were the flirt, Laouise O'Mara. Kicking up your legs on the swings, so all the boys could get sight of your drawers!'

There was a snort from beside her. 'And you always the jealous one! Sour face and scraggy pigtails. Clodagh Murphy, fishing for the boys but never could catch one! And you a grown woman now and still green-eyed. And all because Father O'Brien's been giving me a bit of the silver tongue, the old goat.'

The two exercise bikes whirred faster.

'Sure, and I'm beginning to fry! The sweat's running off me!' Sister Theresa's black veil was unpinned, the white linen headdress deftly removed, both draped neatly over the handlebars.

'Jesus, Mary, Joseph and all the Holy Martyrs!'

Sister Theresa caught the stricken gaze. She smiled

wanly, putting a hand to her balding head, the sparse grey tufts of hair… 'It went, Clodagh, me lovely mane of hair… years ago. Patrick….he died, would you know? Japan it was. He loved that country so, he never did come home. The Japanese Water Garden, Clodagh – all that planning, the long hours? It was all in memory of me darlin' boy…'

Sister Mary slid from the bike and adjusted her skirts. She took up the dangling garments from Sister Theresa's bike and held them out. 'There was only the one boy for me, Laouise. But he never did have eyes for me…' She huffed. 'Me of the sour face and scraggy plaits.'

But there was something else. That hair, treacle gold it was. She'd been hot fire with jealousy; burned with its festering. And all these years…Patrick O'Mara…and his sister's golden hair…both gone. The waste of it. The sacrifice…

Sister Theresa clambered down from her bike. She replaced her white headdress and pinned on her veil. The two women moved sedately out of the gymnasium into the sunshine, their robes brushing softly together.

'And if you're going to start harping on again about me and Father O'Brien, Sister Mary, there's no need.' An indignant flounce of skirts. 'I'm casting me eye elsewhere. There's this very nice young curate…got an arse on him as round and as tight as a peanut…'

The Sisters' voices faded in the direction of the Japanese Water Garden…

Barbara Featherstone is an 'Essex girl'. She was born in a maternity hospital in Epping Forest, once a TB convalescent home built on the former site of a 'lunatic asylum' where, for some years, the poet John Clare was a patient. Barbara now lives in a century old Dorset cottage with her husband and their cat Captain who thinks he's a dog.

She has combined her passion for writing with a teaching career in primary schools and bringing up her three children. She writes fiction for adults and children. Her short stories have been published in national magazines. She has been short and long-listed in several competitions, including BBC Radio 4's Opening Lines and *Mslexia*. Her children's novels have been Highly Commended.

Barbara is a keen member of a local creative writing class tutored by the novelist Ian Burton. She is currently editing her children's fantasy novel which gives her the pleasurable ability to inhabit two worlds at the same time.

SHORTLISTED
ALISON FISHER

Nothing Stays the Same

I was watching a line of geese low and heavy in the sky when the girl screamed. She had been following us since South Norwood Lake, even climbing after us through the gap in the fence into our road and I thought she must have caught herself on the wire. But she was pointing at our flat, at the frantic flurry in the living room window.

'What was that?' she blurted. 'On the window sill.'

She put her thumb in her mouth and darted accusing glances from me to Robyn to the half-open window, empty now, except for the red sun shining on the glass. Robyn let out a nervous giggle and said, 'So?' I can guarantee my sister will always say the wrong thing at a time like this.

I leaned down to the girl — she was from Robyn's class but small for her age — and said, 'You're weird. Everyone says so. No-one likes you.'

She stepped back as if I'd hit her.

'Go on, clear off.'

She shot off down the street.

'Idiot,' I said to Robyn. But she made like she was deaf and headed into the block. As usual, old Mrs Sullivan was on sentry duty in her second floor doorway.

'Is your mother all right Tara?'

'I can go to the shops for you,' I told her. My mother used to help decrepit neighbours with their shopping. Mrs Sullivan wasn't grateful though. She sagged, drawing her coat together with one speckled hand, the other clutching a paper bag.

'But where is she, Tara?'

'She's good,' I said, but she still creaked after us to the stairwell, watching till the turn took us out of sight.

The flat was cold because of the open window. I was sure I'd told Robyn to shut it. Dad's toolbox was still in the cupboard under the kitchen sink, and I got out a hammer and nails. The living room window frame is wooden so it wasn't hard to hammer it shut. The branches of the trees were almost bare and I could see Mrs Sullivan make her way to the little park opposite our flat. She lowered herself onto a bench, opened her paper bag and hurled crusts at the pigeons.

Robyn was sweeping sunflower seeds off the sofa. When she realised I was looking at her she said, 'I want to visit Grandma.' She's been banging on for days.

'I told you. There's no need.' I took the hammer back to the kitchen and got the last of the fish fingers from the freezer and put them in the oven. Robyn came in and dragged a chair along the floor to the cupboard. She climbed up and got out the money tin. We both knew how much was in there, but she held it to her ear and shook it, and then counted it out loud on the table.

'D'you know, Tara,' she said, pretending to be surprised. 'There's enough to go to Beckenham.' And I just couldn't be arsed to argue any more.

We hadn't told them we were coming and Grandma was flustered. 'I don't know what I've got to feed you.' We said we'd had our tea, but she went into the kitchen anyway. Grandad was looking out of the window, as that's where his chair points. Grandma brought in a tray with a plate of shortbread and a teapot under a cosy, and once she'd poured the tea we told her Mum had changed.

She said 'Changed?'

We said, 'Yes, she's changed.

'Not herself?'

We said, yes, you could say that. She's not herself. Grandma glanced over at Grandad, who was gazing at the launderette and the chemist, and then she leaned towards us, lowered her voice and said, 'It's her age. Some women do. At her age. I expect she's going through the change.'

And we said yes. She's certainly going through a change.

We helped carry the cups and plates back into the kitchen and she came to the door with us and kissed us goodbye.

On the train home Robyn made a big thing of putting her arm round her sketchbook to hide what she was drawing. Mum was an artist but when Dad left she said she couldn't afford the studio any more. Of course, Robyn has decided she's an artist too. After she learnt about perspective she went round everywhere holding her pencil up in front of her pretending to measure things until it got so annoying I broke it in two.

She was given a sketchbook on her seventh birthday. It was the day we went to the Museum of Local Artefacts and Natural History, where birds and animals stand round in their own skins pretending to be alive. Robyn marched around the glass cases looking for victims. It turned out to be the arctic terns' lucky day. Two terns perched on papier maché rocks looking bored to death. It was hard to believe those birds, before their insides turned to wool and wire, had flown halfway round the world. Most of the birds there were brown and grey, like old people on buses in winter, but the terns had bright crimson beaks, the same colour as the lipstick Mum always wore. Mum stared at a photo display of baby blue tits in a nest, with her head cocked to one side, a way she had even then. A board on the wall said: 'Their mouths are brightly coloured to attract attention,' as if you could miss it. That's all they were, mouths stuck onto balls of fluff. Bright yellow mouths stretched open in rings, blind bulging eyes, little bodies swelling picture by picture until the last one, a nest bursting with hunger.

Dad came over and his leather jacket creaked as he put his arm round Mum's shoulders. She stood there for a moment, then she shifted away, and he dropped his arm back down to his side. Robyn ran up waving her drawing. Her tern was lopsided, like she'd started at the beak or the tip of a wing and worked inch by inch from there. Mum took the pencil and in two minutes she'd sketched the terns. Not in detail, only in broad strokes, yet they were so real I was frightened to look away in case there was a whoosh of feathers and if I looked back the page would be blank.

As the train pulled into Crystal Palace Robyn flipped her sketchbook closed and clasped it to her chest. I waited till we'd reached the top of the metal bridge that crosses the rails and then I grabbed it.

'Give it back,' she shouted.

I pushed her off and flicked through the pages. Every one was covered in birds or parts of birds: eyes, wings, beaks and claws.

'This is sick,' I said. 'Even for you.'

'So?' She tried to look down her nose at me, which meant tilting her head back. Without even thinking, I threw the book over the parapet. It hung in the air for a second before it fell, its pages whirring. Robyn stared at the parapet as if she expected the book to bob back up again, and when it didn't she started to cry, but no-one took any notice.

Though it was dark, the bars and restaurants and take-away places were busy. Robyn scuttled ahead of me and when I caught up she walked faster, so I did too. She crossed over to the other pavement, and when I crossed over she crossed back again. So we walked in parallel lines on opposite sides of the road. At the corner of the library I stopped to look at London, lit up below, and when I turned back I couldn't see her anymore. Outside the supermarket people were milling round with bags and shopping trolleys. I called her name. I started to run, round the corner and down Church Road. She was there, sitting on a low wall outside a white block of flats. As I got nearer I could see a small black coin on her knee, shining in the streetlight.

'I fell over,' she said. 'I knocked my scab off.' She slid off the wall and took my hand.

Mrs Sullivan is never in her doorway after dark, but we could hear her TV. Our flat was so silent when we came in, for a moment we thought Mum had gone. She wasn't splashing in the bathroom sink or perched on any of her usual places. We finally found her in a new bed she'd made for herself in the airing cupboard.

Mum has always been small. She used to buy clothes for herself at GapKids, and force complete strangers in supermarkets to pull down packets of cereal from high shelves. Perhaps that's why it took me so long to realise what was happening. I picked her up – she weighed almost nothing – and carried her to her room. She hopped onto her bed and tilted her head, darting glances around. She had stuck photographs of us into the frame of her mirror, and I went and looked.

We are in the park in front of the Museum having a picnic, all four of us, so I don't know who took the picture.

Me and her are feeding the ducks at South Norwood Lake. She is looking at the camera, (I am concentrating on throwing bread to the ducks) and laughing. I am much younger and she is pregnant with Robyn.

Something fluttered in the mirror. It was her, perched on the top of the wardrobe. Had she flown up there? Could she do that now? She'd had dark hair, and in the bedroom light her feathers had the same blue black sheen.

The phone rang. Grandma calling to see we'd got home safely. Robyn rushed in, holding the phone out.

'It's her mother,' she whispered.

'Who?'

'You know. The girl.'

She pushed the phone at me.

'Hello?' I said.

'Is your mother there?'

'Yes.'

'Can I speak to her?'

Mum edged along the top of the wardrobe.

'I'm afraid she can't come to the phone right now.'

'I want to speak to her.'

'Well you can't.'

I waited and she said, 'Tell her to call me,' and hung up, which I thought was quite rude... Robyn was hovering beside me.

'What'll we do when she calls back?'

'She won't.'

'She will,' she said, her voice getting higher.

'She won't.'

'She will.' She was working herself up. Once she starts, she can go on forever.

'Like some hot chocolate?' I said. She followed me into the kitchen and sat down at the table where she keeps her drawing pads and her pencils all lined up in height order and sharpened to points. I spooned hot chocolate into mugs. She was drawing feathers, filling them in with tiny pencil lines.

'Why?' I said. 'What good does it do?'

She pretended not to hear.

'Stop it. Stop drawing birds.'

She mumbled something.

'What?' I said.

She looked up at me, an appeal in her eyes. 'I can't stop. I have to draw them.'

The microwave dinged. We drank our hot chocolate, and when we had finished, Robyn took the mugs to the sink and washed them up. We cleaned our teeth and went up to our room. We got into bed and said goodnight.

We are awake, listening to the fluttering and soft thumps like something bumping into furniture. When I woke up this morning I held my breath in case the warbles from the trees outside our window were met by an answering call from inside the flat. The noise is worse in the summer, but I think only the stragglers are left now. In the museum there is a photograph of men with funny moustaches, wearing enormous wings made of real feathers. They didn't understand they would always be too heavy to get off the ground. Birds are designed to fly; their bones are hollow, their skeletons only webs of calcium and air.

I once told Robyn that at night, when the museum was closed, the arctic terns came out of their case and at daybreak they went back to their frozen poses. I laughed at her when she believed me. She said how do you know they don't? And I said they don't. And she said how do you know? And I said I just do. She kept on. But how? How do you know? On and on and on. Until all I could see was the birds of the Museum slowly circling in the musty air, the dim glow of the spotlights on their glass eyes.

Robyn murmurs and turns in her bed, asleep. And I wonder. I could take the hammer from its place under the sink, but perhaps this time use the other end to prise the nails out of the wood.

Alison Fisher was born in Baltimore, USA, and grew up in London. She has two children and lives in Brighton. For many years she has been a TV scriptwriter. She won the Bridport Prize in 2010, has had a story broadcast on Radio 4 and a flash fiction in *The Stinging Fly*. Currently, she is continuing to write short stories and is starting a novel.

Lucy Luck commented:

'The voice of the narrator is very well done – both she and her sister are consistent and convincing, and I like the way their situation – mother turned into a bird – is drawn out through the story.'

EAMONN GRIFFIN

Eighty-six Teaspoons

An electric frizzle. Polly opened an eye. First, nothing but haze. She blinked the distortion away. Paisley. Red and blue swirled patterns from a past generation.

Polly shoved the material from her face. She rolled over, sat up. She'd fallen asleep on the sofa then. It hurt when she yawned. Her cheek felt rippled; cushion imprint.

The curtains were open. She must have left them that way. She hadn't intended to sleep. Just rest. For a minute.

A second yawn. This one sprayed saliva. There was a word for that: gleek. She'd just gleeked. She should change her name. No longer Hopkins, but instead Polly Gleeker.

That brought a snicker, and the little laugh made her cough. She gagged. She didn't puke as such, but sat on the edge of the sofa coughing and retching until the queasiness went away.

She wiped her mouth with something. Something paisley. His pyjama top. The top from the set they'd giggled over in John Lewis.

The upcoming first stay in hospital had meant they'd had

to go and buy him some pyjamas, so they'd gone and got the nuntiest pairs they could find.

Nunty. That was another one of his words. He was full of them. Words. To be nunty was to be unfashionably old-fashioned. Dowdy, a little scruffy, mildewed. You knew nunty when you saw it.

The pyjama top now had a wet stain. If she washed it, it wouldn't smell of him anymore. That was why she'd curled up with it, wasn't it?

She'd never get that smell again. He'd smelled of outdoors and cleanliness and musk. Like sex in a forest.

The room pulled away again. A Hitchcock distortion effect: she tracked out and zoomed in simultaneously. When the bolt of nausea passed, she used the top to wipe away tears.

She was crying. He'd have said something else. Bealing. Bealing what was little kids did when they didn't get what they wanted.

She was a kid now, she supposed. All alone and no-one to look after. No-one to be cared for by. No-one to care for.

She found her specs down the side of the sofa. She put them on.

The television was on. So that was the electric sound. Dust motes swirled above the set like lazy flies. The telly was old: the cathode ray type. A dusty grey box in the corner of the room. They'd been meaning to get a flat-screen one, but could never quite justify the expense. It worked fine as it was.

The sound was off but the subtitles were on. A geezerish bloke snarking at a run-down kitchen. An unkempt garden. Now, an auction house. More chirpiness. Bidding and pointing. A silent hand falling, a gavel cupped within.

How long had she slept?

Polly checked her phone but the screen was dead. She'd plugged it into the charger, but it was off at the wall. She switched it back on and tried to stand. There were bottles and a glass at her feet.

Being upright wasn't so bad.

But being upright wasn't the problem.

Polly did the things that grown-ups were supposed to do. She had a shower and brushed her teeth. She pulled on a fresh vest and some loose summer trousers. She tied her hair up and went back downstairs barefoot.

The empties went in the recycling. She stacked the dishwasher. One plate. Wine glasses. A mug. Some cutlery. The big knife that she used for most kitchen jobs. She cleaned down the surfaces. She put a wash-load on. Changed the kitchen roll. She fed the dog.

She put the milk back in the fridge.

There wasn't much inside the refrigerator. Two bottles of his posh lager. Three different kinds of mustard. Chilli sauces. The cheese he loved.Loved.

She didn't stop crying until the fridge was empty and its white walls and wire shelves smelled like the hospital.

Polly knelt in front of the fridge and rested her head against the door. The machine's humming was like bees. A hive for little electric bees.

And then her phone rang. It would be spasming on the hardwood floor, singing and vibrating, dancing to its own tune. She let it go to message, and then she went through to see who it had been. It was from HR at work.

She'd send them an email back after five thirty. After they'd gone home for the evening. Yes, she was fine. No, she wouldn't be in till Monday. Yes, she realised that would take her over her allowance of compassionate leave days, and that she could elect to either have the time off unpaid or deducted from her outstanding holiday balance. Take it off the holidays please. See you Monday.

There was a second message. It must have been left when she was in the shower, or else while the phone was off. She listened to it twice. So that was it. All ready. She could collect any time she wanted.

Now a soft crumpling sound from the hall. Post. There might have been three days' worth there. Pizza flyers, a parish newsletter, cards. She sifted the cards out, put them to one side. She'd send replies after.

After she'd done what needed to be done.

The dog padded through into the kitchen. She heard it drink, but it didn't bother with the biscuits.

'Come on, Blue,' Polly whispered to the red-rimmed reflection. 'You can do this.'

That had been his name for her. A local thing, he said. A term of endearment, like "duck", "love" or "pet". Blue.

Polly put sunglasses on to go out. An old pair. One of his. She found them in the glove compartment. Other things: loose CDs, a tin of sucky fruity sweets, crumpled diesel receipts.

She drove into town.

It was weird being around so many people. Dozens of them, then hundreds, all of them tidal against her, pushchairs and walking sticks and motorised scooters and wheelchairs. Their faces were animated, blurred, discordant. Accents, laughter, chuntering, sneezes.

Polly went to her own bank, but any would have done. Her armpits were prickling. She stood in the doorway, breathing deep. The door swung open without her touching it. It must have been on a sensor. She gave herself time to calm down. It's only people. You used to be good at people.

The world was smoked and blurred. Why hadn't she found her own sunglasses? The prescription ones? Then she would have had a reason to wear them. Sorry, I'm a little long-sighted. And I broke my others. She got what she needed and then got out of there.

Then the pound shop. She wasn't sure how many she'd need, so she guessed at a hundred. You got three for a quid, but even so, it felt foolish. Thirty-odd pounds spent in a pound shop. 'For a party,' she said, as the assistant bagged them up, like she needed to give an excuse to buy stuff.

'Big party,' the assistant grunted. 'There you go.'

It turned out that she wasn't far off.

Polly got everything on the kitchen table, poured herself a glass of wine, and stared at the box. It wasn't much to look at. The kind of thick cardboard box you might find an old camera in. This was what she'd collected after she'd left the pound shop.

Bollocks to this. Bollocks.

Polly drank.

Then she opened up the container from the Crem.

Inside was a sealed bag, about halfway in size between a sharing packet of crisps and a kilo of sugar. The sort of bag you stored excess spag bol sauce in the freezer with. A printed white box to scribble on something to identify the contents. It was filled with a grey dust. She was expecting the dust to be fine and smooth, like sieved flour. It wasn't.

Hopkins. Written in capitals, but with a dot over the i. A blocky hand, as though the author was more used to writing signs for market stalls.

Polly gulped the wine. Then she poured herself another.

She got out what she'd fetched from the bank, a rubber-banded bundle of the little plastic bags you get change in. She opened one and put in a heaped teaspoonful of the grey dust. Then she tucked the bag's closure in on itself and repeated the process.

She kept at it until her wrists started hurting.

That was when it hit her.

For the last couple of weeks, and really in the final days when she'd been sleeping in the hospital, Polly had been living off canteen-bought sandwiches, cups of machine tea after hours. She couldn't remember the last time she'd eaten anything hot that wasn't toast.

Polly found some more wine and went without food. The fridge was still empty. It still smelled like a hospital. A ward's no place for dead things.

She unplugged the machine. The fridge shivered and shushed.

Polly finished the bagging in silence, and then found the stapler in the back of the junk drawer.

She clipped a pouch to each of the near-identical items she'd bought in the pound shop. There were eighty-six in total.

It was getting dark outside. Polly gathered everything together — it took two trips— and put them in the back of the car.

It was a long drive to where he'd come from. Four hours, if the app on her phone was right. How many glasses of wine had she had? Three?

Three would be OK. Just this once. She'd get coffee when she filled up. Keep the windows open. She'd play his music loud. It'd be fine. And besides, there'd be the dog for company.

Polly drove carefully to the beach; out by the yacht club, where the Humber estuary has always met the open sea. Here on the East coast. This was where he'd proposed to her.

She edged down the slipway onto the beach. She killed the lights to make it even more night.

Three a.m. just gone. It'd be getting light soon. Already the sky was fading. Black was becoming violet along the horizon line.

No buzzing out here. No electrics to speak of. Just the wind-chime sound of breeze in the rigging from the yacht club boats. They'd talked about maybe getting a boat.

Polly opened the boot. One by one, she unfurled the Chinese paper lanterns; the ones with her husband's ashes stapled to, then lit the weird squares of fuel-impregnated card, and waited for each to inflate.

Lights twinkled on the far side of the estuary. Out to sea you could just make out the gas rigs. Closer up, the blocky concrete twins of the wartime sea forts. They'd talked about getting a boat out to them once, but had never done it.

So many things they'd never done.

Since his parents had died, they'd had few reasons to make the journey up, and so they eventually stopped. But he'd made her promise to make this last trip.

She was doing this at least.

She let the lanterns go, one by one as they were ready, until they were all free.

The dog roused himself. He pattered down to the water's edge and was gobbled up by the night.

Only then she looked at the purple sky; studded into infinity with a line of creamy-gold commas.

Water sounds; tiny waves falling over themselves to make the shore. Erratic splashes from the dog's disruption of the mathematics of flow.

Polly tuned the aural out. She became visual.

She stared until her eyes played tricks on her, the stream of lights doubling and separating with each blink.

Then she stared until there was nothing to feel except her single heartbeat, and nothing to see apart from the stars going out and the purple sky fading into blue.

Eamonn Griffin lives in Lincolnshire. In the daytime he lectures in creative writing, screenwriting, English Literature and in media theory more generally, and at evening and weekends he makes up stuff and then writes said stuff down. On Saturday mornings he helps to sort out book donations at his local Oxfam shop and will refute all insinuations of cherry picking the best items for himself.

Eamonn blogs at www.eamonngriffin.co.uk and may be found tweeting at @eamonngriffin

LEDLOWE GUTHRIE

Guy Ropes

The road began to slope and the sea appeared as George rounded the corner of the lane. The white on the black. The black opening up to let the white foam through. He sat on a bench for a moment and watched. There was a full moon up there somewhere. He thought about Carol, curled up in her sleeping bag, foetus-like, with an easy conscience. He'd heard gentle snores through the tent wall while he was outside with mud and grass between his toes, tightening guy ropes and securing pegs.

It had all started this morning when they were still at home, sorting out the camping gear.

A drip from his collar rolled down his neck and brought him back to the present. He walked on towards the beach beneath the pale glow of the streetlights. As he got closer to the sea the clouds began to clear and the rain subsided. The tide was out and he climbed down the damp steps onto the sand, took his flipflops off, and rolled up his pyjama trousers.

George felt very comfortable on the deserted beach. This was the right place to mull things over. Squatting down, he leant back on a big rock, feeling its clammy cold permeating his body. He took out his tobacco pouch to roll a cigarette.

'Hello,' said a voice.

The boy was right beside him, pulling apart a deckchair. George didn't answer, but glanced sharply at him.

'D'you want to sit on this?' asked the boy.

'No,' said George.

It had been buried in the back of his mind for years. And now...these niggling thoughts. Just as they'd come away to relax.

The boy struggled with the deck chair then squatted beside him.

'What're you thinking about? I'm ten and three quarters. I saw you on the campsite. Did you see me?'

'No.' George turned away and looked up at the sky. He just wanted a quiet nighttime stroll to the beach and he'd been tracked by a ten year old. He took out a Rizla, held it between scarred fingers and thumb. He gently put one corner of the paper between his lips while he opened the tobacco pouch and took a good pinch of Old Holborn. The flimsy paper fluttered slightly. George retrieved it and carefully placed the tobacco in its centre. He gripped it before pushing the pouch back into his pocket. He had a lifetime of cigarette rolling experience. With both hands he skilfully rolled a thin white reefer.

'I like the way you do that,' said the boy. 'Can you teach me?

'D'you smoke?'

'No.'

'Not much point in you learning if you don't smoke.'

'I could try it.'

George handed over the roly. The boy held it clumsily, put it to his lips, sucked, then coughed out a cloud of smoke.

'That's very irresbubble of you,' he said.

George looked back at the sky. 'Irresbubble. I like that. It suits me,' he thought.

'Do you know the names of the stars?' asked the boy.

Inhaling deeply George thought about his years out in the back garden or camping up at Seahouses with 'The Sky at Night' and Patrick Moore.

'No. But you mean constellations,' he added with irritation.

'I know loads. Orion…The Big Dipper…mmm.'

Actually, George didn't know much about stars although he usually noted in his diary the dates of eclipses or those unusual events. He remembered that time Carol and he were first married, they'd gone to the beach to watch a falling meteor shower. They'd wrestled in the damp sand for a while before lying back getting cold, waiting for the meteors. (Carol was always convinced that was where she got her cystitis from. George had said that she probably got it from Gordon Dixon and she was lucky not to have got anything worse).

George frowned at the boy. He wasn't supposed to be there.

'What's your name?' he asked, with some resignation.

'Daniel, but I like Dan…Hey what're you doing?'

George was walking down towards a wide stretch of shingle. He really just wanted to think, not talk.

'I'm going to build a tower.'

'Can I help?'

George paused. He was just a boy. He didn't mean to be annoying. 'Why don't we each build one? We can see how different they are.'

'Cool,' said the boy and picked up a huge stone. He struggled, carrying it down near to George and dropped it with a crash to the ground, then walked away for another.

George took a measured approach. He chose each stone, stroked its surface with his thumb, turned it over and over in his hand, feeling the weight and shape before delicately balancing it on the tower.

George didn't want to answer any questions. And he didn't want to think about his years in the butcher's shop. He needed to think about his life with Carol in their semi, with three cats, and a shed at the bottom of the garden.

He thought back to the 'incident' at the hospital. He and Carol hadn't worried. They were only going for a pregnancy check, but later, when the doctor stepped out of surgery, George knew there was something more. The cyst was enormous. There was no baby. George wept as he took the pen and signed his name at the bottom of the form, giving permission for the NHS to remove his wife's womb.

They'd carried on, worked hard, saved wherever and whatever they could. A comfortable retirement was just around the corner and they were looking forward to spending time together, doing more walking. Maybe get a dog. Maybe do a cruise.

But now, with this, there could be a spanner in the works.

'Aren't you going to tell me *your* name?' The boy was back, watching him closely.

'It's George.'

'George,' he repeated. He screwed up his face and continued. 'Do you know why adults can't just be straight about things?'

'What do you mean?'

'Well, you just want, "Yes you can," or "Yes that's how it works," but you always get these long speeches.'

'Well,' George began thoughtfully, 'I think that life starts off very black and white, and the older we get the greyer it gets.'

'You see!' cried the boy. 'That doesn't *mean* anything!'

'Of course it means something. It doesn't mean anything to you, that's all. You'll understand as you get older.'

'So one day it'll be clear to me that life isn't clear?' The boy was pleased with himself.

Frustrated, George handed the boy a stone. 'Here, try this one.'

The boy moved away again, the sound of stones clattering followed. The sea was coming in, eroding sandcastles, moats and boats. A small wave broke with regularity at the points where rocks had jutted out of the water.

It had always been anonymous. That had worked just fine. Once a month down to the clinic, ten minutes in a room with a handful of porn mags. There were nights when he couldn't sleep so he'd work out in his head how many times he had donated. It was like counting sheep. Repetitive, hypnotic. Addictive.

He looked at the boy. They could be related. At a stretch. Same colour hair, similar build, almond eyes. A liking for the beach at nighttime.

'I think I've finished mine,' said the boy. 'What d'you say?'

They both sat down, on cold stones, staring at the towers, and on, out to sea.

'It's good,' said George. 'You've got some natural talent there.'

'But yours is better. You've got loads of little stones, I couldn't make mine balance like that.

'Ah but you've taken more risks, you've got the beginner's luck.' George smiled.

'Let's see which one the tide washes away first.' The boy pulled up his hood.

'Why do you want to do it?' she'd challenged him in the beginning, eyes narrowed

He wasn't sure how to explain without hurting her more, 'When you and I are gone, I want there to be something of me left to carry on. I don't want to be the end of me, I want to live on somehow.'

He knew she didn't understand, and they each had to deal with their sadness in their own way. But he knew she'd seen this biological need gnawing away at him, and she told him to do what he needed to do. She didn't want to know anything more about it.

'Thank you George,' the nurse had said the last time he went in. 'You've made a huge difference to a lot of people's lives over the years.' He thought she was going to kiss him, but she was just doing her job. She shook his hand and opened the door for him to leave. That was it, he'd reached that limit of ten live births; they didn't require his services any more. He ought to have felt some pride, but as he walked away a sense of bereavement descended.

'Look at that,' cried the boy.

A starfish, thrown up by the sea, was helplessly waiting for a wave to catch it and return it to safety.

'They can grow legs again you know. Sometimes they even grow two when they've only lost one.'

The boy was excited and moved towards the starfish, but the sea washed it away before he could reach it.

After a while, he didn't miss it. He kept himself busy. Years of fishing, bowling, cycling. Whittled wooden sculptures filled the shed, and the garden exploded with produce and flowers all year round.

But he started thinking about it again when the computer arrived, along with spam email. He ignored sites like 'Goldenballs', but finally emailed a professional sounding company.

'Have you got any kids?'

'No. Not really,' he said shortly.

'See you've done it again. Do you mean yes or no?'

'It's a sort of; one of those grey areas I mentioned.'

'Oh you've got step kids.' The boy was pleased with his deduction. 'I've got a stepbrother. He's well annoying.'

'Really?' George took his tobacco out again.

'So, how old is your step kid?'

'I don't know…and it's not a step kid…Don't you think

you should go back to your tent now? Someone might be looking for you.'

'No. They never look for me. I can look after myself.' The boy raked up a handful of stones as he stood up, then picked his way to the water's edge. The waves lapped over his feet and slowly crept up his legs as he took aim and threw each stone out to sea.

'Irresbubble,' George thought.

The courier had turned up at the back of the butcher's one warm day last spring to collect the sample. The kit had been delivered to the shop and he'd just been waiting for a call to say that the specimen was needed. The toilet had a lockable door, but it didn't have the same impersonal feel to it as the clinic. Coats and bags hung on hooks. An old lipstick lay in a puddle on the back of the sink. Two torn bus tickets and a couple of paperbacks collected dust and urine stains on the floor. It was an altogether seedier feel than that of the clinic. He had self-consciously handed over the specimen ten minutes after he'd produced it, then slunk back to the counter to finish slicing the gammon.

Waves crashed around the boy's solitary silhouette.

George shouted, 'Dan! You're going to freeze!'

Dan didn't move. George rolled his pyjamas higher and waded out to stand beside the boy; clothes clung to his childish body, his face was soaked. George put his arm around Dan and squeezed his shoulder, feeling his ribcage shuddering in and out.

'Hey. Maybe we should be getting back. It's starting to get cold now.' George had to shout over the waves.

The boy looked hopeful and wiped his nose on his sleeve. 'Can we do this again tomorrow?'

'Yes,' George nodded, 'I like the sound of that, Dan'.

They were sorting out the tent pegs when he saw it on the doormat. His name. His address.

'....I knew I should have destroyed it', she had written. 'But I couldn't. I saw it as my luck changing.'

George knew it was a mistake. That was all. A bit of paper on the ground, dropped by a courier. It wasn't really anyone's fault. But the woman had kept it. She only wanted to be able to tell her child who its father was. He couldn't deny her that. But he needed to break it to Carol. Who knew what this could mean? He wouldn't disturb her now but there were an awful lot of things he needed to talk to her about. Better start with a cup of camping tea in the morning.

They crossed the beach and paused at the bottom of the steps.

'Let's wait a few more minutes,' said the boy.

The two figures stood, not quite touching, facing the sea. They didn't speak. They just watched the black of the sea breaking into chaos, as it washed over their piles of stones, until there was no trace of them at all.

Ledlowe Guthrie studies Writing at Sheffield Hallam University. She won first prize in the Off The Shelf Competition for a poem commemorating their 18th Birthday, her play 'Graveside' was performed at The Lantern Theatre, Sheffield and her short stories have been published in: the 2014 Sheffield Hallam Anthology *Matter, The Pygmy Giant, The Front View, Ink Sweat and Tears*, and she was longlisted for the 2014 BBC Radio 4 Opening Lines competition.

Ledlowe works with older people, takes photographs, and mooches around in woods, cemeteries, beaches and disused areas of the city, just so long as there aren't many people around.

SHORTLISTED
SOPHIE HAMPTON

Ghost Bike

On the night of Ella's funeral he takes her bike apart as
carefully as if he is dismantling her bones. He works in the
tiny garden, with the light from a torch and a sliver of moon,
watched by two foxes from the roof of a shed. He takes off
the basket and the water bottle and the bell. He releases the
wheels. His fingers numb with cold, he removes the chain and
the cassette. When he disconnects the brake cables he stops
and closes his eyes, listens to the rhythm of the restless city.

He cleans and degreases and oils before he reassembles
the parts. He uses an aerosol spray to paint the bike; the
solvents make him gag but he keeps his finger lodged on
the valve until the can is empty and the transformation is
complete.

He picks up the water bottle. His hands are oil-black
flecked with white, like the clear night sky. He unscrews the
lid, put his lips to where hers have been and drinks. When the
foxes howl he howls with them. Chinks of yellow appear at

neighbours' windows. A baby cries.

He wheels the bicycle to the junction where she was killed. He takes a black sack from his pocket. The detritus of the roadside memorial angers him. He gathers armfuls of rubbish: decomposed flowers; rain-sodden bears with hearts on their bellies; flaccid helium balloons; cards: *in* sympathy, *with* sympathy, with *deepest, heartfelt, sincerest* sympathy; a graduation photo, warped and faded, in a futile plastic wallet; a plywood crucifix, flat on the ground, criss-crossed with the prints of tyres. Using a heavy chain and a padlock he fastens the bike to the railing at the side of the road, drops the key into a drain.

He visits the bike when he can't sleep, which is most nights. So late that the sky has surrendered its blackness to the deepest purple. He can see the bike from a hundred metres, after he turns a corner. It gleams under a streetlamp, whiter than the yellowed hue of bone or the bluish tinge of skin in shock, morphed into the skeleton of a large animal: humerus, femur, pelvis. When he visits the bike he has to lean against the railing to steady himself.

The pavements are empty. He looks up as night buses rumble by; he studies the silhouettes through steamed windows: bodies slumped, sleeping after a late night out or before an early shift. The ground judders when lorries pass, when wheels meet pot holes. He tastes the diesel in the fumes. The trees are naked but for Christmas lights which sparkle as though a million glowworms crawl the branches.

He touches the bike's cold frame or places his hands over the handlebars, grips the rubber so tightly and for so long that his knuckles glow under the streetlamp too.

One night it snows: fleet London snow, dusk till dawn. Those who wake late will witness only salted slush. The quiet of the muted traffic makes him uneasy. When he turns the corner he cannot see the bike. He runs towards the crossroads, as fast as he can without slipping; the bike remains camouflaged until he is a few metres away. He leans over the railing to catch his breath. Tears pockmark the snow at the edge of the kerb.

'How old were you when you learnt to cycle?' Ella called, the wind blowing her cape of curls, her skirt folded up and tucked into the waistband so that the hemline rested on her slim thighs. Her heeled boots slipped on the pedals and she stuck out her legs in a V. 'I learnt when I was four!'

'And only took off the stabilisers last week!'

She laughed and rang her bell. She had fallen off her bike a year ago — braked too sharply, skidded. The thud of her body hitting the ground had made his stomach lurch. Since then she had always ridden in front. 'I'm fine,' she had said, jumping up. 'How embarrassing. Don't make a fuss.' Grazed palms and knees, ripped tights.

Recently he had begun to nag. 'Are you sure it's still okay to cycle? We should get helmets.'

'Me? In a helmet?' she had said. 'I don't think so.'

She pedalled faster as they approached an amber light at the crossroads.

'Stop!' he called. 'We won't make it.'

'Come on!' Ella turned her head to see where he was.

Red. He braked. She didn't. A lorry. Her bike skated along the road as though it was on ice. She was no longer on it. Silence. Traffic stalled in all directions. Drivers leapt from their cars. Crowds formed. People clutched phones, paced.

He did nothing for a few moments, a few minutes: red, red and amber, green, amber, red, red and amber, green, amber … A woman put her hand on his shoulder. A slick of blood trickled from beneath the lorry. The driver stepped down from the cabin, his face as white as the sky. The camber of the road channelled the blood towards a drain. Sirens screamed. Blue lights flashed.

A policeman asked him questions. He didn't watch as the paramedics pulled out her body. She had countless broken bones. Her bike was unscathed.

They had seen their baby at the twelve-week scan, white on black: the spine, the nasal bone, the jaw. Six centimetres long, crown to rump. The next day, after work, in a bar with red velvet seats, he told his lover that he could not see her again. He had to, once he had seen the baby's bones, its head, its bottom, two hands, two feet ... He talked to his lover in the bar and later, after she started to cry, outside where the wet cobbles reflected the orange streetlamps. She lit a cigarette, blew the smoke into his eyes. 'I pity your baby,' she said, words enunciated, lips pale.

When he got home, Ella was asleep on the bed. Phone in hand, boots and coat discarded on the floor. In the light from the hallway he watched the rise and fall of her belly, out of sync with the tick of the clock. He clenched his fists, swallowed.

Ella stirred, opened her eyes. 'What time is it?'

'Quarter to nine.'

'How many have you had?'

'A few.'

'I thought we were both doing this. The not-drinking. The not-smoking. The everything else.' She sat up. Switched on the lamp. Her eyes gleamed glossy as liquorice. 'What happened to our night in?'

The smoke on his clothes did not mask his lover's scent: citrus and spice. He took off his jacket. 'Sorry.'

'Who were you with?'

'A couple of colleagues ... Ella?'

'Yeah.'

'I'm scared that I'm not going to be a good dad.'

She held out her hand. 'Come here. You'll be fine. We'll both be fine.'

He sees skeletons and broken bones: in wintry branches; in wax which drips down tall white candles; in the veins, picked out with hoarfrost, of a frozen leaf; in the trails left by slugs on a path; in silver strands hanging from a Christmas tree.

It had been Ella's turn to visit his family this year. He sits, drunk, mute, one of eleven at a table destined for twelve. He eats little, tastes nothing. His sister's baby sits on her husband's knee. When his nephews snap the turkey's wishbone he swallows the vomit before it leaves his mouth.

He picks up his plates and cutlery. In the kitchen he dislodges meat and potatoes from a bed of gelatinous gravy before scraping them into the bin. He stands at the window, studies the gleaming wet paving slabs and roofs and chimneys. The branches of a beech tree sway against a mottled sky, bushes quiver. A watering can tumbles across the garden, hits the wall.

From the dining room the baby cries: he flinches at the lusty screams. Raindrops splash against the window. He pictures Ella's eyelids on the evening she told him, so purple and swollen that for a moment he thought she had been attacked. Her fingers trembled as she smoked, sprinkling ash onto the duvet. He glanced at the vintage champagne on the bedside table. The lamp shone through the bottle, cast a glimmer of green light on the wall.

'Sorry,' she said. 'It's all there was to drink.' She rummaged under the pillow, drew out a plastic stick, passed it to him. 'It's not too late. It's nothing yet. Nothing at all.'

He swallowed. 'How far along?'

'Eight weeks. Ish. It's not a baby.'

'No.'

'It's not even a fetus till nine.'

'You don't want it.'

'I didn't say that. I've just found out. I don't know.'

He sat on the bed. Lit a cigarette from hers.

A gust rips ivy from the wall of the house; the strand flutters and swirls, soars upwards like the tail of a kite.

'You should get a haircut, shave,' says his father, not unkindly, as he is leaving. 'Make you feel better.'

He opens the front door. Contrails scar the sky. He inhales deeply, as though he has been holding his breath.

He receives a card, *Thinking of You*, from his lover. *So sorry* he reads, one kiss. He phones her on New Year's Eve. He gets a haircut, shaves. Unwraps a present he thinks might be a jumper, it is. They meet early, in the bar with red velvet seats; when the conversation wanes he picks at stuffing that spills through a gash in the fabric. Later, perfume chokes the air and condensation trickles down the windows and he can't hear her speak. They finish the second bottle of Malbec, jostle their way out.

He wanders the streets with her. Couples kiss, and more; girls' bare legs blue in headlamps. Drivers honk. Smoke snakes above the huddles outside pubs. A man pisses in a shop front. They pass a nightclub; he feels the beat of the bass in his stomach. The sky glows orange-black. Litter swirls around their ankles. Sirens bring a cold film of sweat to his forehead. He kicks a beer bottle against a wall, enjoys the smash of broken glass. Aims at a second bottle, misses. Fireworks explode. A smell of sulphur on the wind.

When she takes his hand he tries to pull away. She won't let go and he squeezes her fingers so hard that he might fracture her bones. She lets out a cry. He pulls her round a corner, drops her hand to point. 'That's where Ella was killed,' he says. 'Just there.'

'Oh,' says his lover. 'Oh.'

He hears a bicycle bell. He sees a girl sitting on the ghost bike, her cape of curls blowing in the wind. 'Ella!' he calls. He runs towards the bike, awkwardly, in his stiff, smart shoes. She is no longer on it. He kicks the front wheel. He kicks it and kicks it and kicks it until it buckles. He stops. His gasps form clouds under the streetlamp.

A couple walks up to him. The woman puts her face close to his. Her breath smells of onion. 'You're fucking sick,' she says. 'Would you kick a gravestone?'

He steps backwards. 'She's not buried here. It's not the same as kicking her gravestone.'

'Shame on you,' the woman says.

He releases the mangled wheel; he will buy a new one, spray it white.

His lover takes him back to her flat. She makes two cups of tea. They have sex on the sofa.

'Were you thinking of Ella?' she asks afterwards.

He doesn't know if he was or wasn't. He doesn't know which is better or worse, for him or for Ella or for his lover. She turns to face the wall.

The flat is suffused with pale light. In the bathroom he splashes his face, as ashen as the lorry driver's. He goes back to the living room to fetch his jacket. A fly floats in the greasy film on his untouched tea. His lover sleeps, or pretends to sleep: mascara smudged, red lipstick perfect. He puts on his shoes. Rubs at the scuffs of paint.

The streets are quiet. He heads towards the ghost bike but when he reaches the corner he pauses. He turns and walks the other way.

Sophie Hampton was born and brought up in London. Her work has been broadcast on BBC Radio 4 and is published or forthcoming in *Southword, The London Magazine, The Bristol Short Story Prize Anthology, The View From Here, The Yellow Room The Eastern Daily Press and Scribble* magazine.

Competition success includes winning the Sean O'Faolain International Short Story Prize, *The London Magazine* Short Story Competition and the *Eastern Daily Press* Short Story Competition, 2nd Prize at the Wells Festival of Literature, Finalist at the Brit Writers' Awards and shortlistings for Bridport, Bristol, Bath, Fish, Exeter Writers and the Hayward Gallery George Condo Competition.

Sophie has an MA (Distinction) in Creative Writing from Sheffield Hallam University for which she was awarded the AM Heath Prize for best MA submission in 2013. She is currently editing her debut collection, *White Socks and Weirdos*.

Lucy Luck commented:

'This is a well-controlled picture of grief and guilt, unsentimental but affecting. I appreciate the way the scenes are put together, to build the story of what brought us to this point.'

CLAIRE HYNES

In Her Hair

The head lice are back, he says, and his breath, scented with throat lozenges, sweeps such a wind around the two children, she fears they will float off the doorstep into the sky.

She strokes Freddie's helter skelter curls, softer than Hungarian goose feathers; slips her fingers through Joss's mane, embroidered with black sequins. She does not think about returning head lice. She thinks, if she lived with the children in Venezuela in South America, or Myanmar in Southeast Asia, rather than Watford, northwest of London, she would sleep with one eye open to guard against thieves armed with scissors.

Have you checked their hair? Have you checked your hair?

She is about to answer this man, Rufus, the children's father, when she discovers that he has grown. His body, honed through regular bench presses and adorned in a chalk-striped suit, looms above the neighbour's lime tree. His head, adept at spreadsheets and navigation, and any skill he wishes to master, skims evening clouds. What is the use of her discussing nits, or the lack of them? This man's ears furnished with golden strands and situated several miles in the sky, are tuned to the sound of comets criss crossing the globe.

I bet you haven't checked your hair? he says from up high.

Of course, nits have hopped to the children's heads from an obvious location. Dottie's hair, the colour of moonless nights, extends at every possible angle in thick coils, and provides luxurious accommodation for the most discerning louse and his extended family. Ten million nits might be crawling through the bushland, sipping Bloody Marys from her scalp, and no-one would be the wiser.

Their hair needs to be checked twice daily, he says. Their hair needs to be treated with Lice-Off or some such noxious substance, which must be left on for eight hours, or preferably their whole life. It does not matter if the Doctor said Lice-Off is ineffective. What does the Doctor know about malathian, dimeticone, isoprpylmristate or cyclomethicane? That hippy-dippy Doctor, with her talk of plentiful conditioner and fine metal toothed combs. What does she know about anything?

A passing aeroplane buzzes before his nose, and he bats the aircraft out of the sky.

Look at Rufus's children down below, such miniscule beings. And Dottie, too. He could lift a foot and stamp the woman into the hall floor, sanded and varnished by him and him alone. Better still, he could empty a barrel of Lice-Off over her culinarily-challenged, navigationally-impaired head. Her unruly hair would dissolve. Her lumpy body would shrivel. All that would remain, in a steaming heap, would be her fat-girl jeans and tee-shirt and her shabby M&S underwear.

Freddie itched the back of his head. Didn't she see? That's where the nits form their biggest community. Right at the back, near the nape of the neck. They march from their settlement across the top of the head in lines, depositing saliva and shit along the way. They stop on the hour, every hour, to feed on blood, before laying a fresh batch of nit eggs. In fact, this minute, he can see, with his telescopic vision, a flurry of the pests about his boy's head, leaping from strand to strand. But this woman, their mother, is so clueless she would not notice.

Dottie ushers the children inside. Freddie's soft curls and Joss's embroidered mane, which may be crawling with nits – although, she thinks not – brush against her hand, as they pass. She pushes the front door closed. Thank goodness. Oh, praise the Lord, she thinks, although she is not religious. But the praise of thanks and the thanks without praise are premature. She is tossed backwards, the door is flung open and a polished loafer of monumental proportions crashes into the hall.

I suppose you've received the letter?

She may have received a letter, or she may not have. She does not wish to discuss what she has received with the man she once promised to have and to hold, in times of nit infestation and nit absence.

Somewhere in the belly of the house, Freddie and Joss emit piercing squeals. Perhaps they are playing on some screen or other, which she will switch off, when bedtime approaches. Rufus, squats down in a fruitless attempt to peer past his foot, and see what Dottie is allowing or not allowing the children to do. The children make too much noise, because she cannot control them. Furthermore, she tells them "no" because she controls them too much. She tolerates behaviour which should not be tolerated and challenges behaviour which should be tolerated. And if she was to tolerate behaviour which should be tolerated and challenge behaviour which should not be tolerated she would still be wrong.

This woman, Dottie, who lacks parenting skills and indeed any number of skills and talents including fine art, picks off the shelf in the hall her most treasured paintbrush, made from sable. Raising the brush above her head, she reaches up

Rufus's trouser leg between hairs the size of branches. Brush connects with anklebone and she hears a thunderous yelp. Tickled foot withdraws and, at last, Dottie slams the door shut.

In the kitchen, she slices apples for the children's night-time snack. She notices, but does not read, the letter propped beside the ticking clock.

Reference Number: ABCDEFGNOWAY00

Dear Mrs Wetherall,

FACCCU (Families and Children Courts Communication Unit) has been asked by Watford County Court to provide it with information following an application that has been made by Mr Wetherall to remove Freddie and Joss from your care. Mr Wetherall has filed the application as a result of an alleged failure on your part to consider Freddie and Joss's health and hygiene, and their physical and emotional wellbeing, and he believes that the children should reside with him.

Mr Wetherall has stated, in his application to the court, that:

i/ When you lived together as a married couple, you failed to check the children's hair for signs of head lice daily at 08.00 hours and again at 19:00 hours as requested by him. Mr Wetherall was therefore forced to assume responsibility for twice daily nit checks. He also carried out associated household tasks to deter the pests, such as washing bed linen and, on one occasion, vacuuming the living room floor. He cites these actions as evidence of his role as the children's primary carer.

ii/ You routinely asked Freddie and Joss to eat vegetables against their wishes, and on occasion, you served lentils at the dinner table. In calling upon your children to maintain such a fibre-rich diet, you inflicted upon them physical distress.

ii/ Your refusal to allow the children to play computer games before bedtime caused them emotional trauma.

Our role is to promote and safeguard the welfare of children who are the subject of family court proceedings. To do this, we need to provide information to the court to help it decide who Freddie and Joss should reside with.

Before the first hearing, we will write a letter to the court (called a 'Schedule 2 letter') outlining the results of the work we have done so far to carry out necessary hair and other checks on your children. A social worker will contact you about this shortly before your first hearing.

Yours sincerely,

Mr D. W. Sterne
On behalf of FACCCU

*

Reference Number: ABCDEFGNOWAY00

Schedule 2 Report for FACCCU (Families and Children Courts Communication Unit) concerning Mr Rufus Wetherall and Mrs Dorothy Wetherall and their children Freddie and Joss.

Mr Wetherall appears to be a highly responsible parent. In the first instance, it should be noted that he is almost bald. Therefore he cannot possibly pose a risk, with regard to passing on head lice to the children. Mrs Wetherall, on the other hand, possesses a mass of hair, inherited from her own mother, who hails from a faraway tropical island rife with hairborne diseases.

Mr Wetherall's nit-staking talents appear to be unsurpassed. When he lived with Mrs Wetherall, he regularly worked his fingers through his children's hair, in search of wingless insects. During the Easter school holiday last year, he found a scattering of white eggs no bigger than pin heads, fixed close to the children's scalps. A considerable number of live head lice were also discovered. No doubt these creatures were transferred via head-to-head contact with Mrs Wetherall, for the reasons stated above.

Mr Wetherall sprayed a quantity of Nit-Off onto the children's hair and left the chemicals to work overnight. Mrs Wetherall was instructed merely to rinse off the treatment the following morning, prior to the school-run. Over the weeks and months which followed, Mr Wetherall repeatedly and tirelessly applied Nit-Off treatment to his children's hair twice daily. Mrs Wetherall protested on numerous occasions that the children were nit-free and that the chemicals found in Nit-Off, namely malathian, dimeticone, isoprpylmristate and cyclomethican, risked causing neurological problems and seizures when applied frequently. It should be noted that Mrs Wetherall's knowledge of the sciences is limited and that her initial response to the nit infestation was merely to apply hair conditioner and make use of a nit comb.

In an effort to limit the damage allegedly inflicted on Freddie and Joss as a result of Mrs Wetherall's irresponsible approach to the children's physical health, food consumption and recreational activities, Mr Wetherall took measures, which included:

i/ Contacting social services to report Mrs Wetherall's failure to instigate daily hair checks.

ii/ Cutting up Mrs Wetherall's bank cards to prevent her from buying food stuffs harmful to the children.

Iii/ Alerting police to the emotional deprivation suffered by Freddie and Joss since their access to social activity, in the form of computer games, was restricted.

Mr Wetherall and Mrs Wetherall's marriage broke down irretrievably in July last year. Mr Wetherall had expressed annoyance at his wife's irresponsible actions most vehemently and Mrs Wetherall subsequently contacted police and claimed that physical violence had occurred. No witness statements were provided to support Mrs Wetherall's claims.

FACCCU actions:
I can report that our researchers have scraped Joss and Freddie's scalp and hair with a no. 15 scalpel blade for investigative purposes. Samples, which may or may not prove to be nit eggs have been sent to the FACCCU scientific laboratory for independent verification. Evidence in the form of a 500 gram packet of brown lentils has been collected from the property where Mrs Wetherall resides. A television, laptop computer and tablet retrieved from her address, will be analysed by the FACCCU IT department.

Mrs Wetherall has so far declined to be interviewed and a further report will be produced in due course to the court.

Mrs K. Stone
Social worker on behalf of FACCCU

It is a bright Spring afternoon, the day before FACCCU is to due to present its preliminary findings to the family division of Watford County Court. Dottie packs into her bag her sable paintbrush and the children's favourite story book and walks to the school. The iron gates are shut and the home time bell has not rung, but the teachers don't object. Yes, she can take Freddie and Joss early.

She runs with the children to a park where small frogs play in long grass and spins them giddy on the roundabout. Afterwards, they sit surrounded by chirping crickets, under the tangled branches of an oak tree and she whispers a secret into their ears. When no-one is watching Dottie scoops up the children and tucks them into her hair.

Dottie strolls through the streets of Watford, towards High Wycombe, with her children balanced on her crown. She sings about an old woman who swallows a head louse and the children laugh at their mother's song and the bumpy ride, and they breathe in the smell of her hair scented with rosemary oil. Dottie sees ahead of her nits, thousands of them, marching in lines along the pavement. Where the lice are going, and where she is going, she doesn't know. But she understands for the first time, that the nits are her friends.

Claire Hynes was awarded a PhD in Creative and Critical writing from the University of East Anglia. She was singled out for recognition by the David Higham Associates literary agency while studying for an MA in Creative Writing at UEA. As a freelance writer, Claire contributes to national publications including *The Guardian, New Statesman* and *Mslexia.* She has won a George Viner Memorial Award for Journalism and is a director and editor at Gatehouse Press. Claire is working on her first novel.

Photograph by Mark Tillie © 2014

SHORTLISTED
K LOCKWOOD JEFFORD

Clairol Perfect 10, 9A

I've dyed my hair blonde and I'm wearing dead-trendy leggings and a belt round my waist 'cos I read in Take a Break that makes you look slimmer. I've lost nearly two stone. Catching sight of myself in shop windows I think, you look all bleedin' right you do, better at 30 than you did at 20. Nearly as nice as Dr Di. (She don't know I call her Dr Di. I don't to her face.) Dr Diana Miles can afford good clothes, like I bet she goes to Jigsaw or Karen bleedin' Millen. I have to make do with Primark or charity shops. Dr Di's a model for my new look. So is Hazel who works down the chip shop, though I ain't been there lately 'cos of the diet.

Dr Di's my shrink. I see her on a Friday once a month at my GP's surgery. I've asked her no end of times if I can see her more often but she goes no 'cos she's only there once a month. I could see her more if I went to her clinic at the hospital but I've told her no way am I going there. It's full of nut-jobs.

Today's Thursday and I'm on my way to the caff for a bit of breakfast and a fag. Obviously I have to go out for the fag. As I go in some heads turn to see who it is. Or to make sure whoever it is shuts the door 'cos it'd freeze your tits off outside. Inside it's dead cosy and smells of bacon.

I hear that pasty-faced Eileen go, 'Here comes Loopy Linda.'

'You're one to talk,' I go. 'If you say that again I'll smack you in the mouth, alright?'

'Ooh, I'm scared,' she goes, and that daft sod Derek, who she's been leading on, giggles, all in with her like.

He'll never get his leg over that frigid cow. I suck my teeth as I pass them, like I learned off Winston, the security bloke down the YMCA gym.

'Don't take no notice Lindy love,' Rosa goes from behind the counter. 'What you having today? Usual?'

'No, I'm still on a diet, Rosa,' I go, ignoring the sniggering behind me. 'Got another half-stone to go. I'll just have a cuppa and one toast with a scrape of butter.'

'There'll be nothing left of you,' goes Rosa, wiping the counter with a damp cloth that looks like an old pair of Y-fronts. 'Mind you, you don't half look nice with your new hair.'

'Ta,' I go. 'It's Clairol Perfect 10, 9A. They don't do it in the Chemist by me, I 'ave to go all the way to bleedin' Islington. Ooh, sorry. Slipped out.'

Rosa don't like swearing in her caff.

She tuts, but not about me swearing, 'Annoying, innit?' she goes. 'I hate it when they don't have your colour.'

I stare at the back of her head as she sorts out my tea and toast. Her crown is a grey circle, and her purplish crinkly hair spreads out from there.

'Your roots need doing, Rosa,' I go. 'Want me to do 'em for you?'

'You're alright, love,' she turns and hands me my tea. 'My Eric does the back where I can't reach. You sit down. I'll bring your toast.'

I pick a table by the window so I can see out. If I don't I get clos. That's short for claustrophobia. It's loads better now. I used to have to walk in backwards and shout what I wanted over my shoulder.

Rosa's put too much milk in the tea but I don't say nothing 'cos I don't want to upset her and have Eileen going all smarmy. I'll give her, 'Loopy Linda'. She's the bleedin' one needs her bleedin' head examined.

'Rosa,' I go, turning round.

'Yes love?'

'D'you mind me swearing in my head?'

'No, you're alright, love.'

I shoot Eileen a daggers look. At least I'm trying to sort myself out, seeing a shrink, trying to be more normal. I've never been normal, always the odd one out. At school I used to run round the yard shouting to imaginary friends 'cos no one ever picked me to play with. I got sacked from lots of jobs except when I was on the game. The money was good and it's the only way people like me can get sex. A lot of the clients liked me because there was plenty to grab hold of. Not anymore. I've no intention of going back on the game again. I want a proper job. That's why I'm going to see Dr Di.

I talk about things with her and she teaches me stuff. Like what I think is going on in people's heads might not actually be what's going on.

Last time I told her about this old geezer who was walking slow with a stick on the pavement in front of me, taking up all the room. I didn't want to be late to see Dr Di so I went, 'Scuse me,' and squeezed past him.

Only he went 'Arsehole' and when I looked back he was waving his stick in the air.

So I went, 'I'll knock you over the head with your bleedin' stick, you old git.'

Dr Di went on about how I could've handled it differently, how he might've been frightened when I pushed past, how he could've been shaky on his feet, how he was an old man and not a threat to me blah, blah. Well, she wasn't bleedin' there was she?

I tried to change the subject only she kept going back to the old geezer 'til it got on my tits and I shouted and she went, 'Lower your voice, please.'

That wasn't a good session. I came out all wound up.

She makes me laugh sometimes. Like once I told her I liked her boots. They were nice, came up just over the ankle, with a heel. She didn't say anything. I knew she wouldn't.

So, I go, as a joke, 'What size are you?'

She goes, 'Why d'you ask?'

That's something she does. Asks me why I'm asking whatever it is. Never a straight answer. Drives me mental.

So I go, 'So I can nick 'em off you if they're my size. Are you a 5?'

She goes, 'I wonder if you want to be in my shoes?'

That's another thing. She's always going on as if everything's about her.

I always go, 'No, I wasn't thinking that.'

But it doesn't stop her.

Another time she was 10 minutes late. I started talking straight-away so's not to waste time, about my mother being late picking me up from school. Once she didn't turn up at all. I had to wait with Mrs Elmore who was all frowning and sighing, checking her watch and looking out the window, hoping she wouldn't have to take me home with her. When my mother eventually turned up she smelled of gin already. After that a lady social worker started calling 'round the house asking questions. Like how did Linda get a bruise on her cheek? And what did Linda have for breakfast? I knew the answers (I fell over and chips) but she wanted my mother to say. The lady social worker took me to a Wimpy Bar and goes 'Call me Melanie, you can trust me' and everything. She didn't even have enough money for a coke-float after going I could have anything I wanted! She didn't last long, anyway. After her there was a man social worker who put his hand on my leg instead of the gear-stick when he picked me up from school.

I asked my mother if I could wear trousers when I had to see him and she went, 'No. I'm not getting into more shite with the school because you're a fuss-arse.'

She was bitter and twisted 'cos Dad ran off with the next-door neighbour who was miles prettier than her. She never wanted me anyway, only had me to look after her when she went doolally. I was glad when she died of gin poisoning, even though the social workers put me in a kids' home, Nazareth House. Nazi-house we called it. I wanted to be adopted but the social workers went, 'No-one adopts teenagers.'

After I told her all this, Dr Di went, 'I wonder if you're anxious I'll forget you or reject you.'

Honestly, you couldn't make it up.

I've thought of asking Dr Di what she uses on her hair. Clairol Perfect 10, 9A, is the closest I've found to her shade. I wonder if she has a bloke to do round the back. I won't bother asking 'cos she definitely wouldn't answer. She wears a wedding ring so she must have a bloke. Unless she's a lesbian. Sometimes I wish I was lesbian 'cos I have no luck with blokes.

'What bloke would have you, damaged goods?' my mother used to say.

Don't know what she meant. Dad liked me. When she was making our tea in the kitchen, he used to cuddle up and lick my ear and whisper how he couldn't wait to show me the facts of life. He used to pull away when she came back in and wink at me. It gave me a funny feeling, like scary and exciting. When

I was on the game I used to hope he'd show up, then I'd show her who'd bleedin' have me.

I've tried to make friends but I end up with the rubbish people no-one else wants. Like I tried to be friends with Eileen when I first met her at the cheap Aqua Aerobics class, the one for old-ies and us on the dole. I invited her to my flat, made Nescafe Gold Blend and got digestive biscuits in and everything.
She took out a pack of fags so I went, 'You can't smoke in here.'
'Open the window,' she went.
'No. You'll have to go on the balcony. Even I smoke on the bal-cony, and it's my bleedin' flat.'
Well she got the 'ump and left. Now she calls me Loopy Linda.

Dr Di keeps going on about group therapy. I've told her I'm not going in a bleedin' group, sitting in a room with a bunch of nutters going blah, blah, I'm mental. No, I'm trying to be more normal.

'You finished?'
Rosa's standing by my table with the Y-fronts in her hand again, smelling of bleach.
'Yeah, cheers, Rosa,' I go, and hand her my cup and plate.
I hope she's not offended I left half the tea. If she is she don't say nothing.
'See ya later,' I go. 'I'm off to Islington for my hair stuff. D'you want anything?'
'No, you're alright, love.'

It's a bleedin' crush on the tube. I'm by the door and there's this teenage boy and girl. She's very blonde and I'm wonder-ing if it's natural or Clairol. The tube lurches as it comes into Angel and I bump into her.
'Sorry, love,' I go.
She narrows her eyes and the boy sucks his teeth.

'I said sorry,' I go, again.

They ignore me. I think about what Dr Di might say about why they're acting like this. Maybe they're deaf? When the tube stops I can't reach the doors 'cos these two are in the way.

I go, 'Scuse me, it's my stop.'

They don't move so I go, 'Scuse me, I got to get off.'

They still don't budge and when the doors slide open they get off. Why they didn't just say they were getting off too is beyond me. I step off. They wait and start walking behind me.

I hear the boy suck his teeth again and the girl go, 'Bitch.'

I turn round and go, 'Bitch yourself.'

The boy grabs my arm. I try to get him off. The girl swings her bag at me and it hits me in the shoulder. I go backwards and, to stop myself falling, I grab at the nearest thing. A handful of her blonde, bobbed hair. Only I carry on going backwards because it comes off in my hand. All of it. I land on my bum with her hair in my hand.

She's screaming, holding her hands either side of her bald bonce, going, 'The bitch took my wig.'

I chuck it to her, only the tube's going out the station and a whoosh of wind blows the wig onto the track. I don't hang about to see what happens next.

No, I'm legging it up the bleedin' escalator, thinking, 'What will Dr Di say when I tell her tomorrow?'

No doubt she'll think of something.

Originally from Cardiff, **K Lockwood Jefford** lives in London and Folkestone with her husband and works in the NHS. She has always written but started writing short stories 'seriously' after completing a part-time course in creative writing in 2012. Since then, she has had a couple of stories published in anthologies and is part of a small writers' group that meets fortnightly. Her ambition is to have more time to write but for the time being she writes some evenings and most weekends, either at the kitchen table in London or from a second-hand desk with a sea view in Folkestone.

Lucy Luck commented:

' Impressive 1st person voice, well-controlled, allows us to feel how complicated the narrator's life is, and how she manages to control herself within a world that doesn't understand her or the rules she needs to live by.'

KAREN JONES

Teodor's Boots

The pawnbroker's wife had more jewellery than she could ever hope to wear and his son more toys than any child could play with. The pawnbroker had nothing but his longing for Teodor's boots.

When Teodor first brought the boots to the shop, the pawnbroker undid the elaborate knot in the string that held the lid onto the box and examined the boots carefully. The box was tatty but the boots were heavy, steel-toe-capped and the soft black leather shone under layers of lovingly applied polish. They agreed a price and a time limit for redemption. Teodor came back the day before his time was up and bought the boots back. He did this several times a year for two years.

The pawnbroker stopped examining the boots after the first few exchanges, just accepted the box from the big calloused hands and stacked it on the shelf at the back of the shop. It would be there just long enough to gather another thin layer of dust that would settle into the grime it wore like a winter coat. He and Teodor had fallen into a sort of friendship – the closest the pawnbroker had ever come to such a relationship – and they would drink sweet tea, often laced with something stronger, and chat while the shop was quiet, Teodor laughing and smiling as he told stories of his work and his workmates. The pawnbroker had never performed manual labour, had never had workmates, had never known anyone as big and loud and funny as Teodor.

One day he asked Teodor about the boots.

Teodor's voice softened. 'They were my brother's boots. He died in the yards. I got the boots; my father got his coat and his debts. Father wanted to sell the boots but I wouldn't let him. I needed the boots for work, so I could bring money into the house. He let me keep the boots if I took on my brother's family. So, I married his wife — it was no hardship, as she is a great beauty, some say the most beautiful in our town – and I raise his three fine sons. We moved here in hope of a better life. I bring you the boots when I have no work lined up on the docks, I buy them back when I know I'll need them. The boots are what hold it all together.'

The pawnbroker didn't know how to respond. 'I'll get you a new box. Something so precious should be better cared for.' He started to untie the string.

Teodor stayed his hand. 'The box was my brother's. The boots and the box stay together. And anyway, it's not the box that matters; it's what is inside that must be taken care of.'

The pawnbroker nodded. 'I'm sorry, I had no right. It's not my business.' He walked to the back of the shop and placed the box in its usual place. 'See you in a few weeks!' he called, but the bell above the door was already ringing Teodor's departure.

The pawnbroker was surprised at his own envy. In wishing for the day Teodor would fail to find work and not redeem the boots, he knew he was hoping for another man's misfortune, a man he thought of as a friend, but his livelihood depended on misfortune, his price tags lay on other people's misery. He convinced himself he was a lifeline, not a vulture.

In the gloomy apartment above the shop his sickly son,

who could not go outdoors because of allergies and a weak immune system, looked out at children playing in the street. He knew his son would swap all his toys for one day playing outside. And his wife, who stayed at home to look after their son, would swap all her jewellery for one night out at a restaurant or even just for a walk in the park. She'd swap everything she had for a walk in the park with her son.

And he would swap them both for Teodor's boots. He caught his breath, shocked at his own thoughts. Why those boots? He could buy a pair the same, but Teodor's boots had been walked in and worked in and lived in. And what work – real man's work. He would feel as big and strong as Teodor if he had those boots.

Alone in bed that night – his wife had taken to sleeping on the floor of their son's bedroom – he thought of Teodor's words: The box doesn't matter – it's what inside that has to be taken care of. He woke to his wife and son talking softly in the living room. They did everything quietly, like visiting mice afraid to disturb the homeowner. He longed to be woken by laughter and life.

The next time Teodor stopped long enough for tea and chat, he turned the conversation to the pawnbroker's life and family. The pawnbroker was ashamed as he told this big man with the beautiful wife, fine children, work fit for a strong man, of his own weak son, timid wife, lifeless apartment. He told him how he envied him his work, his life.

Teodor shook his head, smiling. 'You are a different kind of man. I work in all weather, any work I can get, but with my hands. My head is not so good for work. When I work my head goes somewhere else. It goes for walks on beaches, it climbs mountains, it dances with beautiful women. My hands get rougher, my back more bent, but my dreams stay young and healthy. I'd be no good with figures or thinking. But you – you, sir, are a thinker. The world needs men with brains as much as it needs men of action. We work at what we are good at. We are good men. We provide for our families. How we provide does not matter.'

He looked around the shop. 'If your wife and son cannot get out to enjoy life, then you must take life to them. And you have it all here. So many lives, so many hobbies waiting for the right hands to resurrect them, to save them from an existence behind glass, waiting. No more waiting, my friend.' He shook the pawnbroker's hand firmly, patted him on the shoulder and left.

Later, as the pawnbroker dusted the cabinet of musical instruments, Teodor's words came back to him. Perhaps that was the thing – he could choose an instrument for his son to learn, hire a tutor to teach him. As he rearranged the books he wondered if his wife could have a book group – other women to visit her, an interest to share. And for himself – he looked at the calendar – he would wait for Teodor's boots.

The pawnbroker's son learned to play the guitar and, according to the tutor, had enough musical talent to perform in public. Although everyone knew this was impossible, it brought hope and happiness to the household. His wife's book group flourished and she started to take greater care with her appearance, even wearing some of her jewellery. Soon when he woke in the mornings it was to the sound of laughter and chatter and music.

The pawnbroker no longer thought of Teodor's boots. Now that he had his life back, his family back, he realised that the boots had never been what he wanted. He couldn't wait to see Teodor, to tell him how, thanks to him, he had found the love of his family again.

But Teodor did not return. The pawnbroker waited for two weeks then took the box down from the shelf and set off for Teodor's house.

He had visited this part of town only occasionally, even though it was where most of his customers lived. Barefoot children in threadbare clothes played in the streets, shouting and laughing and happy, seemingly oblivious to their desperate circumstances. He wondered if any of these were Teodor's children and looked for similarities before remembering they were really Teodor's stepchildren. Such a big-hearted, generous soul. His chest tightened as he became more convinced that some misfortune had befallen his friend.

He knocked on the door of Teodor's house. The door was so flimsy he felt it would buckle under even his weak hand. A tiny blonde woman opened the door. She was dressed entirely in black. Her face was scrubbed clean and her skin so white it shone against the darkness of her clothes and her surroundings. She was far older than he had imagined and he was ashamed of himself as he thought, if she was the town beauty, what did the others look like?

The pawnbroker gave a quick bow of his head. 'You must be Irenka. I was worried about Teodor — he didn't come back for his boots. Is he all right?' He looked past her, into the room. 'Did he buy new boots?' he added, hearing the desperation his own voice.

Irenka looked at the box under his arm, then shook her head and snapped at him. 'Teodor died— didn't you hear? No wonder, the way he drank.'

He held his hand to his chest. 'I am so sorry. I didn't know. When he didn't come back for his boots – I know how important they are to him – I should have known. You must be so upset. I know how he loved you.'

Irenka took a step back and regarded the pawnbroker with suspicion. 'Are you mad? Why in hell would Teodor love me? He rarely even paid his rent on time. He had no respect for an old widow like me or for anyone other than any bartender who would extend him credit. What's this nonsense about boots?'

'I don't understand – you are Irenka, yes? His wife? Well, yes, widow. He pawned his boots to provide for you and the children when…'

Irenka grabbed the box from his hands and started to undo the string. He tried to stop her but she shoved him away. 'Boots,' she muttered, 'as if he'd have boots. Or a wife, or children.' She tore open the lid, let out a satisfied, 'Ha!' and showed the pawnbroker the brick that lay inside the box.

The pawnbroker picked up the brick, felt the weight of betrayal in his hands. Irenka handed him the box, indicating a piece of paper that lay inside. 'Look, the old scoundrel has left you a note with your "boots". I wish he'd left me money for his rent.'

The pawnbroker unfolded the note and read: *My friend, I am sorry you have found me out. I am a bad man. A drunk, a liar, a wastrel. I used you, just as I used so many others, to pay for my beer, the thing that gave me something to live for while it killed me, as it must have killed me if you are reading this note. Those first few visits to your shop, I borrowed a pair of boots from a drinking companion, but he changed his ways, put the boots on his feet and took to work. So I started to bring the brick, hoping that by then you thought you knew me well enough to trust me and not open the box. I judged you right – you are a good man and you saw only good in me. I hope you will forgive me. You are so kind. Please believe me when I say I thought of you as a true friend, enjoyed our long chats in the warmth of your shop and your hospitality, and meant no harm. Teodor.*

The pawnbroker looked at Irenka, her hard little face set in a look that said, 'See?' and then he felt the laughter start deep in his belly and roar out into her shocked face. Every time he looked at the brick he laughed. How long he had looked at that box, desperate to untie the string, to own Teodor's life. Teodor's life was, much like his landlady, a hard lump of unyielding stone.

He put the brick back in the box, folded the note and put it in his pocket. He thought he might frame it. He put the lid back on the box and tried to replicate Teodor's knot. He couldn't quite get it but he knew he would spend many smiling hours trying when the shop was quiet. He bowed again to Irenka. 'I am so sorry Teodor owed you money and that you do not mourn his passing. He was a great man — he saved my life and the lives of my family. And if this,' he lifted the box and gave it a gentle shake, 'is all that he left, then he left more than many and better than most. I hope your next lodger is more to your liking and that one day your mouth will remember how to smile.'

He left her standing in the doorway, her sour little face twisted even further, and walked through the streets where Teodor had staggered while spreading his stories, humour and wisdom. His tread felt lighter, the box heavier, his smile as wide as it had ever been.

Karen Jones is from Glasgow. Her stories have appeared in numerous magazines, e-zines and anthologies. She is addicted to short story competitions and has been successful in *Mslexia, Flash 500, Spilling Ink, The New Writer, Writers' Forum* and *Words with Jam* and was shortlisted for the Asham Award. She is also addicted to zumba, yoga and salsa, which are far healthier and stress-free pursuits.

She is currently working on her third novel and thinks this might be the one she actually sends out to publishers and agents. Maybe.

Her short story collection *The Upside-Down Jesus and Other Stories* is available from Amazon.

ANNEMARIE NEARY

Gon-do-la

The foreman looked happy, perched up on the gantry for
the special meeting. Perhaps the target for Golden Pyramids
had been met. Twenty thousand plastic shells assembled,
painted, and adorned with tiny decals. Twenty thousand
pencil sharpeners glued into the base. After a moment or
two, though, he grew impatient — clapping his little hands,
shouting silently against the din of the machines.

Zhang examined her comrades, standing at the fire exit
with the door propped open, sucking deep on their cigarettes.
She despaired of their ridiculous hair, styled into stiff peaks,
their dangling earphones. Dim, she thought. Useless. Nothing
between their ears but guava-scented mousse and loud music.

Someone handed the foreman a megaphone as the empty
conveyor belts flowed on behind his back. Zhang hoped he
had something worthwhile to say. *Production is Glory*, she
thought. *Waste no Breath but for Labour*.

'New moulds have been manufactured,' the foreman
announced, his voice like a quacking duck on account of the

megaphone. 'No more Golden Pyramid pencil sharpeners. From now on, Work Group 25 will be making a model boat.'

An office worker emerged from the deep shadow of the admin building, a man who looked like he had never seen the sun. In his fragile arms he carried a cardboard box, a prototype for the foreman to display. The boat was long and slim, each end tipped up into an elegant swirl; a girlish, fancy thing.

With a smart flick of his wrist, the foreman snapped the hull along its length, two halves cracked clean as a nut. Then the office worker handed up a smaller box, no bigger than a bar of soap. The foreman shook out a handful of plastic figures and tossed them on his palm. 'Man, woman, boatman,' he said. 'One, two, three. Simple,' he said. 'Easy. Gon-do-la.'

The word sounded Japanese to Zhang. She imagined an emperor launching a great fleet: dragon kites overhead, men straining at the oars. But this boat was too narrow for fighting men, too delicate for war. Gon-do-la. The foreman liked the word so much he pronounced it again, stretching the syllables out as far as they would reach. Gon—do—la. He gave a little nod then a flourish of his hand, as if he'd just performed a dance and deserved applause.

The office worker distributed leaflets, shoving them into people's hands whether they wanted them or not. There was an assembly diagram — simple, Zhang agreed, easy — and an illustration of the boats swarming on a sky-blue river that ran through a golden city.

'Picture,' the office worker said helpfully, 'for front of box.'

Zhang peered at the sky-blue river, the golden city. 'Old-time city?' she asked.

'Water-city,' he shrugged. 'Some place where *guilaos* go for love.'

'Not China,' Zhang said.

'No,' the office worker agreed. 'Not China. Italy.'

Zhang had heard of Italy. Ferrari. Maserati. Vroom

vroom. Pizza, Pasta. Eat so good.

'Gucci, Prada, Fashionista baybee,' squealed the guava girls. They wriggled their hips at the office worker as he made his escape.

Although Zhang had heard of Italy, she wasn't exactly sure where it was. Normally, she would have asked her sons, who seemed to know where most places were. But the sons didn't come to eat with her that evening, so Zhang consulted the kitchen wall instead. Recently, the boys had pinned up a laminated World between the blue glow of the fly killer and the tremble of the fridge. They used the map to chart the journeys they would one day make. Lian dreamt of Toronto, Bo of New York, but neither of them had ever mentioned Italy. Zhang narrowed her eyes until finally she found it, so far away she needed both her hands to span the distance.

At the end of the month, the foreman called another meeting at the gantry. Output of the new boat had exceeded expectations, he said, his voice quacking out from the end of the megaphone. Already, the factory was producing more gondolas than any other company in China. It was time to diversify. Three office workers appeared this time, each one paler than the last, each one bearing a cardboard box held out like cake in front of him.

The foreman beckoned the office workers forward one by one. 'First gondola, basic model.'

The guava girls put their fingers in their lips and blew a catcall while the first office worker held the familiar black and gold model up above his head and performed what might be called a twirl.

'OK, OK ,OK,' said the foreman, waving his hand. 'Basic gondola is basic gondola. Now for Deluxe model.'

The second office worker also played up to the girls. He tried a bit of a swagger, dispensed a wink.

'Deluxe model has velvet interior,' said the foreman. 'Integral light.'

The office worker flicked the switch on and off and on

again.

'This is gondola for romance, ' the foreman said. 'For using next to bed,' he explained, flushing slightly.

'Ooh baybee,' the guava girls cooed. 'Sexy time.'

'But finally,' the foreman raised his hand to demand their full attention. 'Fin-al-ly. Work Group 25 will make the Exquisite.'

This model was bigger than the others and required two office workers to carry it. Zhang gasped. It was beautiful — a delicate shell-pink creation with golden swirls and poseable figures. While one of the workers fiddled with a little lever at the side of the boat, the foreman cupped his ear to indicate that the boat was playing music. Even though it was impossible to hear it above the racket of the machines, the guava girls went momentarily silent, as if this gondola was playing all their innermost tunes.

Zhang was put to work on Exquisite, gluing in a boatman and two tiny *guilao* lovers. She sang to herself, gave the little people their very own names. Spaghetti, Margherita, Mafia. As the moulding machines spat out the parts. Zhang glued on trim and sealed the hull. She imagined dramas for the little pale-faced lovers. Plastic-coated desires.

Then came Zhang's birthday. The date flared auspicious red on the calendar she kept taped to the kitchen wall beside the laminated World. Her sons were always generous, but this year they came laden down with boxes. Although it made her stomach ache to see such waste, Zhang decided to be thankful for ridiculous chocolates dressed up like jewels, for electronic foot spas and smart phones, for shiny dresses two sizes too small.

The night before her birthday, the boys revealed another gift. 'Three day holiday,' they said. 'Special trip.'

Zhang was worried – normally a form was required, one month's prior notice given. It was coming to the end of the accounting period and the foreman was a stickler for paperwork. But the boys, so smart these days in their Hong Kong suits, told her that the foreman already knew. He had even requested a photograph of Zhang's trip as a memento for the staff canteen.

There was only one possible explanation: she was about to be awarded a Distinguished Employee Award to mark her forty years of service. Zhang imagined another meeting at the gantry — the presentation of a certificate, maybe even a medal. She visualised the stunned faces of the guava girls when they saw her photograph displayed on the Wall of Supreme Honour, right next to the Cabinet of Productivity that contained all the best-sellers — the Eiffel Tower backscratcher and the Great Wall of China draught excluder. But Zhang had broken her own rule when it came to having expectations, and her birthday passed without any announcement at all.

That evening, her sons were waiting for her at the apartment building. She barely had a chance to wash her hands and face before they insisted it was time to leave. She tucked the metal chairs around the table, transferred the bowl of soaking wood ear mushrooms to the fridge. She folded the laundry into the plastic mesh basket, pulled down the blind. The boys insisted she bring the shiny dresses they had bought her, the shoes that made her toes pinch.

'But dress comfortably for the journey,' said Bo, always the kindest son. 'It will take a little while to get there.'

"The first leg of the journey is by train,' said Lian, who was more practical. 'The second by ferry. It may get cold.'

Zhang survived the tedious train journey by sipping at the lukewarm tea that Bo had brought for her in a lime-green plastic flask. She watched the reflection of her sharp-suited boys in the window as they slapped down playing cards on the flip-up table. Once there had been a motto for every possible situation. Some of those phrases still popped into her head at the appropriate moment. *Capitalism is the Tendency of the Well-Off Peasant* she thought. But there was no point in mentioning that now, not on a birthday trip.

Once they had settled themselves on the ferry, Zhang slipped off into the thick plush of sleep. She dreamed of a cornfield, stretching out in front of her like a vast golden ocean. She could not see any comrades, though there must have been some. All she could hear was the hum of the machines that seemed to harvest the crop without making any impression at all on the sea of swaying corn. It was so calm, that place, so purposeful. But though she could have spent eternity there, that's not what her sons wanted for her.

'Wake up, mother,' said Bo. 'We've arrived.'

People were gathered at the windows, jostling, pointing, chattering excitedly. Outside, the sky was erupting, bursting into chrysanthemums of fire. Zhang had always loved fireworks, but she'd never had them on her birthday before. She joined the others at the window where her sons had elbowed out a space for her. When she peered out into the night she saw that they had reached a kind of fairyland. They sailed in through a golden gate and up a broad waterway lined with gleaming buildings.

'Don't you recognise it, mother?' asked Lian. 'After all those gondolas you've made?'

'It's Venice,' said Bo.

Zhang frowned. Italy was two hands' span away from China on the laminated World.

How could this be Venice?

'Not the old Venice,' sighed Lian, when he saw the look on her face. 'Not the rotting one, the one that stinks. No, no, no. The water there is green and foul. The houses crammed with disregarded spirits. This is the Chinese Venice. All-inclusive. Five star.'

Zhang hadn't realised there was a Chinese Venice. She looked up at a glorious skyscraper, at its flashing golden sign. *Royal Lagoon City*, it said. *Deluxe. Exquisite* *****

'They perfume the water,' said Bo. 'Provide a choice of music through your headset — Crooner or Rockstar, Waltz or

Gaga.'

Lian reached into his pocket and drew out a leaflet. 'See, mother?' he said, thrusting it into her hand. 'In the Rialto Bridge pool complex, the sky is permanently blue. And at the end of every day, there is a perfect sunset. All at the click of a mouse.'

'This is the best Venice,' said Bo.

Her grown-up boys were bright-eyed, awaiting her reaction. Still dazzled by her cornfield, Zhang blinked sleep away. As her eyes acclimatised, she realised the gondolas were Exquisite, top of the range. They were pink. And motorised. And softly lit with cherry blossom lanterns. And there was music, just as she'd imagined it, like a tinkling wind-up jewellery box.

Zhang considered her sons, with their magnificent bellies. She gazed out at the shining tower, the softly gliding gondolas. Bo had his phone out, and was taking her picture from every possible angle. Ah, she thought, allowing herself a sigh of satisfaction, the Wall of Supreme Honour. She imagined the foreman, the silenced guava girls. And then she thought of cornfields and comrades, and marvelled at the strangeness of the world.

Annemarie Neary's short fiction has been widely published in literary magazines and journals in the UK, Ireland and the US. Her awards include the Bryan MacMahon Short Story Award, the Columbia Journal fiction prize, a Wordsonthewaves WOW!1 Award and the inaugural Posara Prize. She has won runner-up prizes in the international Bridport and Fish competitions, the biennial Michael McLaverty Award and the UPP Short FICTION competition.

Annemarie was educated at Trinity College Dublin, King's Inns Dublin and the Courtauld Institute, London. She began writing fiction in 2008 after a career as a lawyer and her first novel, *A Parachute in the Lime Tree*, was published by The History Press Ireland in 2012. She is at final edits stage with her second novel and is working on a third. She lives in London with her husband and sons. You can find her on Twitter @AnnemarieNeary1

Samuel Wright

Charade

At the top Grace scanned the seats. A few doubles were still free. She chose the nearest one to the front. The row before it was filled by a fat backed woman and her fat backed son. The row behind held one man with a skullcap. As she sat, she turned in towards the window.

The bus roared and stuttered. Outside, they passed wide pavements and rough housing. She didn't know this route. Blocks that looked like her own hung gloomy in the dark over Chicken Cottage and Kebab Shack. Girls that looked like her strutted in the shelters, but she knew they weren't the same.

The bus hissed and stopped. A man smiled, briefly, as he sat. She turned back to the window as she felt his weight on the seat beside her. The cold and the damp clung faintly to him, and she felt the breath in him, but they didn't touch. He held himself straight, his feet turned out. He stared down the aisle, chin up.

She stared at the street. Three boys paced, arms swinging,

bouncing with each step. A guy sat on the pavement, legs flung. Two girls stood turned towards each other, leaning towards each other over a cigarette. An Orthodox Jew, in fur hat and black cloak, walked round them. He looked like he should be in a different century, but they didn't even look round. She watched him pick his way down the street, straight-backed and self-contained.

She felt the glass grow warm against her forehead. She shifted.

The man beside her rose and left.

The bus hissed and stopped. Wet air, muddy feet wafted up. The hiss of the doors brought a breath of outside. A clot of noise down there, a clogged shout and hustle. She turned from the window to the stairwell. She felt her teeth touch behind her closed lips. The back of one calf touched the shin of her other leg.

'Jesus!' she heard. And, 'Fuck!'

The broad backs of the woman and her son in front of her strained against the seat. She could see where the rail dug into their flesh. Beyond them she heard the white couple, the guy with the glasses and the scraggy beard and his blonde girlfriend, ease from their chatter.

'Fuck off!'

Grace turned her face to the window and stared hard out. Instead of the dark beyond, her eyes fixed on the rubber seal, the dab of wet in the runnel of it. Her hand kneaded the leather of her bag.

'Fucking cunt!'

Then laughter.

'Fucking dickhead!'

Someone was laughing as they came up the stairs. It echoed and bounced. It filled the whole bus, not just the bit of the bus that was your space or your neighbour's space.

With a crash and a thunder of feet, three men arrived at the top. Young, white, and so drunk you could see it in the way they held their hands. Grace couldn't help looking. She stared from behind the woman's fat back.

The tallest of them was laughing. He looked round, met Grace's eyes over the woman's shoulder. The bus felt suddenly smaller.

'Fucking miserable here, isn't it!'

She felt the intake of breath around her. He was talking to them all. Everyone on the bus.

He turned to his friends. 'We're not going to get this lot playing, are we, lads?'

They stumbled fully up on to the top deck. The tall one's head brushed the ceiling. The air felt damp and close. It occurred to Grace that the condensation on the windows had come from the breath of every person on the bus.

The other two were shorter, heavier, but one had a bright ginger beard. Their voices were neutral. London, but not too much of any one London. They swayed down the aisle, then the tall one sat beside her.

She kept still.

He turned to her straight away, not just glancing, but addressing her.

'You're going to play, aren't you?'

She held her face blank and tried not to meet his eyes.

He held up his hands as if caught out. 'Oh, no, sorry.' He turned to the others. 'I think I scared her,' he hissed in a thunderous stage whisper.

'Let's play,' shouted the bearded one.

The third guy shouted, 'Me! My turn!'

Grace stared out of the window at the street. It seemed further away, emptier. The glass seemed thicker. She glanced at the fat back in front of her instead. She could see something in the shoulders, a tension. She wondered if the fat-backed woman was holding her fat-backed son's hand. She wondered if she was scared.

She blinked. She wondered how many other people on the

bus were thinking what she was thinking.

The third of the men lurched forward to the front of the deck. He leant against the lip beneath the front window, and as he spoke, his eyes rested dreamily on everyone.

'All of you play. You're all playing.'

For a moment, the whole bus seemed to hold its breath. The shifts and noises of it, the rattles, the hum and rush of the traffic – none of it stopped, but instead of being the stuff of life going on, it all became background to this bus that had become a room, and this man at the centre of it.

He placed one hand in a clenched fist in front of his eye, and made a circling motion with the other at the side of his head.

'Film!'

'It's a fucking film!'

The other two shouted with delight, even louder than they had before. Grace turned from the window. She could feel the breath easing all round her, the half smiles half hidden. Charades.

The guy at the front held up three fingers.

'Three words!'

'Three words!'

The guy at the front grinned, a lopsided grin that seemed to leak off his face.

'Uh,' he said, then waved two fingers.

'Second word!'

He looked up. He held his chin.

'Thinking!'

His face cracked in laughter. 'No I *am* thinking.' He did the same pose but more so. 'That's my fucking thinking face!'

He waved two fingers.

'Second word!'

'Second word!'

He bared his teeth and did a cat like swipe with one clawed hand.

Lion King, thought Grace. She loved charades. They used to

play them every Christmas. They used exactly these gestures. The fingers on the arm, the open book, the weird antiquated film camera.

'Gay!'

'Angry!'

'Lady Gaga!'

He collapsed in giggles. Then he waved two fingers. Grace smiled.

'Second word!'

He made the same motion.

'Tiger!'

The guy at the front made a manic face and waved his hand as if to say, go on.

'Zebra!'

'Rhino!'

'Your mum!'

He collapsed in giggles. Then he sorted himself out and, his body tilting more than the bus was, held up three fingers.

'I know it's fucking three words.'

He waved the fingers.

'Oh, third word.'

He nodded. Then he held himself upright and placed two hands, one on either side of his head, fingers splayed like a crown.

Lion King, thought Grace.

'Afro!'

'Alien!'

The guy at the front made a comic gesture of defeat.

'Come on! It's fucking easy!' he shouted to the bus. 'Someone's got to know!'

'The Evil Dead!'

'The Lone Ranger!'

'The Toy Story!'

'That's not the fucking name of it.'

'The Lion King.'

Grace felt the strangeness of the words in her mouth. She felt the attention of the bus blink and focus on her. No one spoke.

'The fucking Lion King!' The guy at the front jumped up and down. 'The fucking Lion King!'

He stumbled and fell in a heap on the floor.

The bearded guy laughed so hard his voice went high-pitched. The tall guy, the one next to Grace, turned to her and said, 'Well done!' He smiled. His face was close to hers, and he looked right at her. She could see his skin, his eyes. He stood and ushered her forwards with a hand. 'Your turn.'

Grace froze.

'You won. It's your turn.'

She felt the bus listen. The white couple turned round.

She shook her head. She gave a nervous smile that pulled her face tight and made her temples ache.

'Go on! You won!'

The bearded guy was standing behind the tall one. His voice was still high pitched although he'd stopped laughing. The tall guy leant forward. She could smell the alcohol on him, but his eyes were warm and funny.

'Go on,' he said, quietly. His voice was just directed to her now, to her alone.

'Oh my God,' she said. Her smile grew wider and she stood up.

'Fuck yeah!' shouted the one who'd fallen over. He'd pulled himself up by the rail over the stairwell.

'High five,' said the bearded guy, with his hands raised.

She high-fived him. She felt a giddy shock at his touch. Saliva rushed into her mouth and she felt on the verge of sickness, but only on the verge, and then it was amazing.

The tall guy leant forward and whispered to her, 'Jaws.' His breath was warm in her ear.

She stepped forward.

The bus hissed and lurched. She stumbled. She felt a heel turn under her, but she stayed upright.

'Fucking awesome!' shouted the bearded guy.

Grace walked another pace or two then stopped and turned. She saw the bus in front of her.

Along both sides, it was close to being full. She saw a man with black face and white beard. She saw a woman with pink dreads. She saw a man whose face looked lined and weathered by years of wind until it had thinned to a bone sharp ridge of nose. On the back seat, in the centre, facing her, a thick-limbed man in a grey tracksuit splayed his legs across the aisle and stared.

'You go girl!' shouted the tall guy.

From here, his face was young and expectant. She smiled, an easier smile. She raised her fist to her eye like a viewfinder, and turned the crank of an imaginary camera.

'Film! It's a fucking film!'

She couldn't help smiling, and then she was giggling too and she saw the knife-edged old man crack a half-smile and the woman with pink dreads grinned at her and she met the eyes of the man in the grey tracksuit and he didn't quite smile but he looked amused.

She held one finger up.

'One word!'

She opened her mouth and pointed at it.

'Deep throat!'

She froze.

'Deep throat! The one with the blowjobs! It's fucking Deep Throat!'

The bearded man was saying it, shouting it, and his face was alive with glee. The cold light of the bus shone flatly on him and he looked like a boy with a fake beard, and his eyes sparkled with the thrill of it.

She felt sick. She felt how white her face had gone. She put a hand to the rail.

They were all laughing, all three of them, and other people too. Beyond the windows the city sparkled darkly past, and she felt for a second like she was standing still and they were all hurtling towards her.

'It's fucking Jaws.'

The three men all turned to see who'd said that. The guy in the grey tracksuit had shifted and sat up, leaning forward on his knees. His face was heavy with anger. Grace looked at him. Her mouth opened to say something but he didn't meet her gaze.

'Hey! Fucking brilliant!'

The bus was quiet. The tall guy was oblivious.

'We're all playing! This is awesome!'

His two friends were silent. The tall guy loped, swaying, towards the guy in the grey tracksuit. Grace felt the cold metal of the hand rail against her thigh, and her hand pulled at her skirt. She sat down, heart thumping.

'Your turn, mate.'

The guy in the grey tracksuit said nothing. Grace stared ahead of her. She couldn't see, but no one was speaking. The music was off. The bus hissed and grunted.

'Your turn, mate.'

There was something in his tone that had changed. Grace let her head turn. She saw them. The guy in the grey tracksuit had stood up. He was tall too. They were facing each other. They were standing too close.

A sharp movement. A small, dense crunch, and the man in the grey tracksuit grunted and crumpled, holding his face. The tall guy turned round and smiled, a star spatter of blood on his forehead.

Grace stared. The faces of everyone else were rigid, staring down. Except one. The guy with the beard was looking right at her. His eyes met hers. They were crinkled at the edge like he was laughing, but his stare was hard and still. His lips moved over a word, blown silently to her like a kiss.

Bitch

Her head snapped back round to the window.

Samuel Wright has recently moved from London to the North East, where he is head of a new Sixth Form in Sunderland. He has previously been longlisted for the Sunday Times EFG Short Story Award, and has won the Tom Gallon Trust Award from the Society of Authors. Last year he brought out *The Marshes,* a collection of stories and images in collaboration with photographer Josh Lustig and Tartaruga Press, and several of his stories are to be found as ebook singles from Galley Beggar Press.